★ ★ ★ ★ *ACT. DANCE. SING. PERFORM.* ★ ★ ★ ★

★ AMBITIOUS ★

A PREMIERE HIGH NOVEL

★ ★ ★ ★ ACT. DANCE. SING. PERFORM. ★ ★ ★ ★

★ AMBITIOUS ★

A PREMIERE HIGH NOVEL

MONICA McKAYHAN

KIMANI
tru
™

Recycling programs
for this product may
not exist in your area.

AMBITIOUS

ISBN-13: 978-0-373-22996-3

www.KimaniTRU.com

Printed in U.S.A.

Acknowledgments

God is the source of my talent and blessings.

For all the young men and women who enjoyed reading the Indigo Summer series, especially my reluctant readers—keep reading! You'll definitely enjoy this new series. Let's take this adventure together. My husband, Mark, makes sure that I have a comfortable environment in which to create my stories. My family is my backbone and motivation. Without the support from you guys, I wouldn't be able to do this. I love you! Glenda Howard, you're the best!

This is for you, Granny. I miss you, but I'm glad that you left me so many little pieces of you. My life is so rich because you were here.

Dear Reader,

I hope *Ambitious,* the first book in the new Premiere High series, will inspire you to go after your dreams, just as Marisol Garcia goes after hers. She's talented—no doubt about it. But isn't it funny how things start to fall apart, just when you think you've got it all together? You would think that auditioning for Premiere High School would've been Marisol's greatest challenge. Not at all. Getting into the tough performing arts school was a walk in the park compared to the Dance America competition.

And Drew Bishop, the guy whose charisma captured Marisol's heart the moment she *literally* bumped into him—well, he's got his own issues. Following his acting dreams over basketball is going to take a lot more courage to pull off, especially when those around him expect him to choose a career in sports.

Lots of twists in this one. If you were a fan of the Indigo Summer series, you'll love this new series even more. The characters are complex and represent different shades and walks of life. You'll definitely be able to relate to one or more of them.

I would love to hear from you! Please visit my website at www.monicamckayhan.com and reach out to me. I also have a Facebook page, a MySpace page, www.myspace.com/myindigosummer, and you can follow me on Twitter at www.twitter.com/monicamckayhan. Let me know what's on your mind.

My best to you always,

Monica McKayhan

one

Marisol

I grabbed a muffin and a banana from the kitchen counter and raced out of the house. It was still dark, just before daylight. It was early, but I wanted to get a fresh start. Auditions were competitive; no time for slacking. My routine was well rehearsed, so I didn't have the butterflies anymore, but I was anxious to get it all over with.

As I turned the corner, headed for the subway station, I caught a glimpse of a man running at full speed past me and down Forty-fifth Street. A blue bandanna tied around his head, he panted and leaned over to catch his breath. I felt a light breeze as another guy, dressed in a gray sweat suit, raced past me also. Another person in jeans and sneakers approached from the opposite direction, grabbed the man and slammed him against the window of Mr. Rodriguez's jewelry store. I thought he was being robbed but quickly realized that he was actually being arrested by undercover officers, dressed in street clothing.

His face pressed against the glass of the window, he yelled, "I didn't do nothing!"

"Shut your face," said the officer as he searched the man's pockets. He checked his other pocket and found all sorts of things—a wallet, a package of gum and other stuff that I couldn't make out.

I approached the scene just as the officer pulled the man's hands behind his back and placed handcuffs on them.

"You ain't got nothing on me!" the guy in the bandanna yelled. "Why're you always harassing me?"

As the officer pulled him away from the glass and escorted him to the police car, the man glanced over at me. His eyes were familiar as they stared at me. I stared back, and it was then that I realized that he wasn't a man at all. He was a boy. Diego. A guy that I'd kissed in the third grade. My first kiss. Diego had spent countless nights at my house. He and my brother, Nico, had been best friends for much of their childhood. For a while, the two of them were headed down the same path, but somehow Diego's path went in a different direction.

As the officer pushed Diego's head down into the backseat of the police car, I watched. His eyes were sad as they stared into mine, and I felt sorry for him. I wished we could go back to a different place and time; a time when we played Connect Four in the middle of my living room floor and tossed kernels of popcorn at each other. Diego was playing a new game now; a game called life. I crossed to the other side of the street and approached the Forty-fifth Street station.

"Five, six, seven, eight…"

A bottle of Gatorade in my hand, I looked on as the

skinny dark girl dressed in leotards and black tights tapped her foot to the beat.

"Again!" said J.C. "From the top."

Skinny Dark Girl positioned herself at the center of the shiny, buffed floors, hands on her hips. When the music began, she instantly started to move, the rhythm causing her limbs to maneuver in ways I'd never seen. She was good. I had to admit it. If my routine was even half as good as hers, I was in—no doubt about it.

Getting in. That was my sole purpose in life—making it into J.C.'s dance class. I'd already made it into the hottest performing arts school on the planet—now it was just a matter of making it into the hottest dance class at Premiere. There were several classes to choose from, but students were busting the doors down just to study with J.C. The Premiere High School of Performing Arts is a place where stars are born. The students who attended Premiere High went on to become stars in the world of performing arts—actors, singers, dancers, musicians. Not everyone gets into Premiere High. The auditions are strenuous, and getting in is just as hard as staying in. Students have to maintain a certain grade point average in core classes— English, math and science—which is just as important as dance or landing a role in the spring musical. Students must be well-rounded and talented. Ordinary students do not exist at Premiere High—only extraordinary ones looking for their opportunity to shine.

As Skinny Dark Girl took a bow and exited the stage,

J.C. motioned for the next person to take the stage—me. I remembered J.C. from the community center in my neighborhood. She was there offering a free dance class to the neighborhood kids. The class was given on a first-come, first-served basis, and kids were fighting just to get a spot. Luz and I had jumped at the chance for a free dance class—considering we were the best dancers in the entire neighborhood. We thought that if anybody was entitled to the class, it would be us. In just a few short weeks, J.C. had given us great hope about our talent. She encouraged us both to audition for Premiere High School's dance program. Premiere was the school where she taught dance and ballet, and she thought we'd make good candidates.

"You're both good dancers," she'd stated, "and with a little work over the summer, I bet you'd make it in."

Luz had this strange look on her face, and on the walk home I asked her, "You *are* gonna audition, right?"

"For Premiere?" she asked as if she didn't know what I was talking about.

"Yes, for Premiere. Didn't you hear what she said? She thinks we can make it in."

"Premiere's not for me. I like my school."

"So you like going to a school where you have to go through metal detectors every morning because one of your classmates might be carrying a gun?"

"It's not that bad, Mari," she said, "and even if I wanted to audition for that silly school—which I don't—my parents would never allow it. They want me to go to medical school like my uncle Marty."

"Isn't Marty a nurse?"

"Whatever, Mari. He's in the medical field. And that's the field I want to be in."

"Is that the field you want to be in, or is that the field your parents want you to be in?"

"Mari, your parents will never allow you to audition for Premiere, either."

"I bet I can convince them," I said. "All I have to do is work on Poppy, and Mami will follow suit."

"It's not the school for me," Luz finally said.

It may not have been the school for her, but it was definitely on my radar and I didn't waste any time taking J.C.'s advice to heart. I knew I wanted to audition.

My knees shook a little as I made my way across the floor and up the wooden stairs that led to the stage. As I stood in front of her, I remembered her words—*with a little work over the summer, I bet you'd make it in.* I'd done just that—made it in. Now if I could just make it into her dance class, I would feel complete. I was nervous but had mastered the art of hiding my fear. And though my heart was beating at a rapid pace, no one knew. I couldn't let them know. When you let people know your weaknesses, they take advantage of it. Keep them at arm's length and they can't hurt you. "Never let them see you sweat" was my mantra. Onstage, I performed a hip-hop routine, making sure my neck snapped back and forth and my hips swayed to the rhythm. My face was serious and my long black hair bounced with each movement.

Long black hair—my greatest asset. It was the one and only trait my mother and I shared. Everything else I got from my father—his dark brown eyes that danced when he spoke and an award-winning smile that made hearts melt. Poppy and I also shared the same views about things. He understood my need to experience Premiere High as opposed to attending public school as my brother, Nico, did. He knew that I was an artist and that I wouldn't fit in at an ordinary school. I needed to be in a place that allowed me to spread my wings. My mother, on the other hand, was the practical one. She feared that a place like Premiere High would strip me of my Mexican-American heritage.

"And what's with this so-called hip-hop dancing that you do?" she asked once in her broken English. "What's the matter with modern Mexican-American dances, with music that you can relate to?"

"I can relate to hip-hop music, Mami," I argued. "I love all music."

It was true. I loved all music and could dance to anything—hip-hop, jazz, Latin—everything. If only my mother could see that. After much convincing from Poppy, she grudgingly gave her permission for me to audition for Premiere High. She was probably secretly hoping that I wouldn't get in, that they'd send me packing to the nice little public school in my neighborhood, where I'd learn

English, math and world history and possibly try out for the cheerleading squad. The cheerleading squad just wasn't enough for me. Bouncing around in a short skirt and shaking pom-poms was not going to help me to become famous. Only at Premiere High did I have a real chance at stardom.

I often fantasized about becoming a star. In my fantasy, I'd be making my way down the red carpet, bright lights and cameras flashing as I made the long walk. I'd be wearing a beautiful gown designed by Vera Wang or somebody, and my shoes would be exquisite. I'd have my hair in a funky hairstyle, and I would blow kisses at my fans who'd be screaming my name. "Marisol, Marisol…we love you!" Then someone would throw me a dozen roses; I'd smell them and then continue to sashay down the red carpet until I reached the reporters. And then I'd wake up and realize that it was only a dream—for now.

After my final move, I smiled at J.C. and took a bow. I hoped that she'd enjoyed my routine as much as the people who sat in the auditorium. I couldn't tell, though, because her face was like stone; no expression. But everyone else in the auditorium was clapping and whistling, and I couldn't help but blush. The sound of it gave me such a rush, a high that I'd never felt before. Even if I didn't make it into her class, I was satisfied in knowing that I'd given my best, that I'd already made it into Premiere.

After thanking everyone, I rushed to the back of the auditorium, pushed the old wooden doors opened and

breathed in fresh air. The pounding in my heart eased a little as I made my way down the long hallway of the school.
My jacket tied around my waist, I wore black leotards and
a pair of pink, turquoise and white high-top Chuck Taylor
Converses. I lowered my head and pulled my hair back into
a ponytail, and just as I looked up, it was too late to avoid
the collision. Slam! Right into the most gorgeous guy I'd
ever seen. I knocked a stack of papers out of his hand and
immediately bent down to help him pick them up.

"I'm so sorry," I apologized, gathered the papers and
tried straightening them. "I wasn't watching."

"Well, maybe you should try watching where you're
going next time!"

"I'm sorry."

"Your clumsiness is unacceptable," he spat. He stood
about six feet tall and had light brown skin and a short
haircut. He reminded me of Terrence J on *106 and Park,*
only a little taller.

"Are you serious? It was an accident."

"You could've caused me injury. In fact my shoulder is
aching a little now." He held his shoulder as if I'd really
hurt him. I was just about to give him a piece of my mind
when he grinned and said, "I'm just kidding."

"Why'd you do that? I thought I'd really hurt your
shoulder," I said.

"Nah, it's cool, see?" He moved his arm in a circular
motion. "I had you for a minute, though, didn't I? You
should've seen your face!" He laughed.

"Not funny," I said and started to walk away.

"Hey, what's your name?"

"Marisol. Mari for short," I said. "And you?"

"Name's Drew." His smile lit up his brown face. "You auditioning for something?"

"A dance class," I said. "What about you?"

In a strange voice, he said, "What a piece of work is man? How noble in reason? How infinite in faculty? In form and moving, how express and admirable? In action, how like an angel? In apprehension, how like a god? The beauty of the world, the paragon of animals!"

It was as if he'd transformed into another person. He was starting to sound like the old homeless man who sat in front of the Chinese grocery store on Eighth Avenue, talking to himself.

"What?" I asked.

"It's *Hamlet*. I'm auditioning for a class in Shakespearean theater."

"Glad you told me…I thought you were turning into the crazy man in my neighborhood."

"You don't know Shakespeare." It was a statement and not a question.

"Not really. I've heard of him, though," I admitted.

"Hey, I'll be done here in a few minutes. You wanna grab a slice of pizza at Manny's?"

"I don't know. My entire neighborhood is waiting for me to come home…to see how my audition went."

It was true. My Brooklyn neighborhood was like an extended family—my friends and their siblings and parents. The Block is what we called the dead-end street where my friends Luz, Kristina, Grace and I grew up since first grade. Though we lived in separate houses, it was almost as if we lived in the same house, because everyone knew everything about everyone else. We shared everything. If someone needed flour, dish detergent or money for subway fare, someone was there to provide it. No one went without anything on The Block. And no one could keep a secret. It you had a secret and you told it to one person, by the end of the day, it would spread like wildfire and everyone would be looking at you as if to say, "Why didn't you tell me first? I had to get it secondhand."

They all had wished me luck on my performance, but I could tell that deep down inside they were hoping I didn't make it in. Especially Luz, Kristina and Grace. There had never been a time in our lives that we'd attended separate schools. We'd been together through thick and thin. Our circle of friendship had withstood the toughest of times— yet the circle had never been broken. Until now. Here I was breaking the circle, and they weren't happy about it. They didn't understand that we could attend separate schools and still be best friends.

"Are you seriously trying to get in?" asked Luz earlier in the summer when I'd first auditioned.

"Of course I'm trying to get in, Luz. And you should, too."

"Never. Premiere High is not my style. But I wish you luck."

Luz was just as good a dancer as me. She'd make it into Premiere High with flying colors, but her parents—who were way more traditional than mine—would never allow her to attend there. They didn't even know she had the moves she did; hip-hop moves that went against her Mexican-American heritage and her Catholic background. It was as if she lived a double life. At home, she was the perfect girl—conservative, respectful and obedient Luz. Away from home, she was sexy-dressing, school-skipping, booty-shaking Luz. In the end, she had given me her blessing. She'd even made me take her rosary beads with me to the audition—the ones her Grandma Consuela had given her before she went back to Mexico.

Drew stood there for a moment, as if he wasn't going to take no for an answer.

"Well, I'm going into the theater. If you change your mind, I'll meet you here in about fifteen minutes."

Before I could respond, he was gone. He rushed into the theater. I peeked inside as Drew made his way to the stage, transformed into this Hamlet character and began reciting his lines. He was good. My mind was saying, *Leave…go meet your friends…you don't know this guy.* But something else was telling me to stay. As I took a seat on the back row of the theater, I became lost in his monologue. And by the time he was done, I was sure that everyone in the room believed that he was Hamlet. He took a bow and thanked the drama instructors. I watched as his lean, long legs exited the stage and made their way to the back of the theater—toward me.

"How did I do?" he asked.

"You were aiight," I teased and laughed as if I'd known Drew for more than just twenty minutes of my life. It felt as if I'd known him forever as he grabbed my wrist and escorted me through the heavy theater doors, down the long hallway and outside into the hustle and bustle of Manhattan's busy streets.

We began our stroll and a conversation that was so interesting that I didn't even realize we were standing in front of Manny's. Drew held the door open and I waltzed inside, made my way to the counter and ordered a slice of pepperoni.

"Gimme the usual," Drew told Manny.

"Hamburger, mushrooms and pineapple, right?" Manny grinned.

"And a large Coke…"

"…light on the ice with a squirt of cherry," Manny said before Drew could finish his sentence. "How'd the audition go?"

"It was cool." Drew was being modest.

"He nailed it," I interjected.

"I know he did." Manny smiled. "He's a great actor. And a great ballplayer, too. "

"Not a better ballplayer than me." A perfectly groomed

blond-haired boy walked into Manny's and started dancing around Drew as if they were playing a game of basketball.

"You can't play no ball, man," Drew teased him.

"I'll take you on the court…one-on-one…anytime, any day." Blond Hair stopped dancing long enough to order a slice of double cheese pizza.

I looked for an empty table in the crowded restaurant. Manny's was the popular hangout for young people who attended private schools in Manhattan, so searching for a table was much like searching for hidden jewels—hard to come by. I did, however, manage to grab one just as someone was leaving. I plopped down in the wooden chair with my back against the wall. The Wall. At Manny's, The Wall was a place where pictures of all the great musicians and artists hung—Frank Sinatra, Louis Armstrong, Duke Ellington. You could look at them all and tell that something was great about them, even if you'd never heard their music.

Drew finally made it to the table carrying two silver trays with our pizza slices on them and set them on the table. Blond Hair was close behind, carrying a similar tray. He pulled up a chair and sat backward in it, the back of the chair against his chest.

"This is Preston," Drew said, "Preston, meet Mari."

"Nice to meet you," Preston said with a smile.

"Nice to meet you, too," I said, and before I knew it, Drew started grilling me about my family and where I'd attended school before.

"What brought you to Premiere?" he asked.

"I took a dance class last spring and was inspired to pursue my goals," I explained. "Before that, I didn't even think that a kid like me—from my neighborhood—could seriously even think about a school like Premiere."

"Same with me. I live and breathe basketball, and in my house there aren't many choices!" Drew explained.

What made you decide to choose acting?" I asked.

"Well, it's still a struggle in my life. I chose acting... but..."

"But now he's gotta tell his dad that he chose acting," Preston chimed in.

"Yeah, telling my dad will be the hard part," Drew explained.

"You guys are brave." Preston grinned and then got up in search of some parmesan cheese.

Being alone with Drew for a moment caused my heart to beat a little faster. As I stared out the window, I felt him staring at me. I wanted to see if he was actually looking my way, and when I glanced at him I realized I was right. He was staring. He smiled and then took a bite of his pizza. Preston returned with a shaker filled with parmesan cheese.

Drew and Preston started engaging in a conversation about basketball, and I found myself wondering what my friends were doing. It was the last week of summer, and everybody in my neighborhood was hanging out—trying to catch the last few moments of vacation. Instead of soaking up some sunshine, I was auditioning for a dance class at the "snooty" Premiere High.

When my phone made a chirping sound, I knew it was a text from Luz.

Where are you, Chica? Her text read.

Manny's for a slice.

Manny's in Manhattan?

Sí.

We're goin to the mall. U goin?

Sí.

Meet us at the Atlantic Ave station in 20.

Bueno.

Order me a slice and I'll pay you back L8R.

Better pay me back.

I promise, I will.

I knew she wouldn't pay me back. She often borrowed my clothes, my CDs and money and never returned any of them. But I didn't mind. I'd borrowed just as many of her things and never returned them, either. We were just that way.

C U in 20. I sent a text back.

I stood and bid Drew and Preston a farewell. "I've gotta go."

"You just got here. Where are you going so fast?" Drew asked.

"To the mall with my girlfriends."

"Wow, dude, we've been kicked to the curb for the mall," Drew teased and smiled that beautiful smile, with the perfectly white teeth.

Something inside of me wanted to know if Drew had

a girlfriend, and before I could process the thought in my head, I received my answer. A dark Barbie-doll-looking girl walked up to Drew from behind and covered his eyes with the palms of her hands. "Guess who," she whispered.

He grabbed her hands; kissed them one at a time. From that moment, I no longer existed. He was taken. Not that I needed a boyfriend, anyway. I was way too busy looking for stardom.

"I hope you get into that dance class," Drew said as he returned from Barbie-doll-land.

"I hope you get into your Shakespearean class."

He stood and surprised me with a hug. "Take care of yourself, kid. And I'll see you at school on Monday."

I couldn't help but smile at the thought of seeing Drew again.

"See you on Monday," I said.

I gave Drew a big smile and made my way to the counter to order Luz's slice of pepperoni.

At the mall, we strolled through Victoria's Secret as if we had money to purchase the sexy lingerie that hung on the racks.

Luz held up a teddy and pressed it against her body. "What do you think?"

"I think this one is sexier." I held up an even skimpier piece of lingerie and pressed it against my frame.

"Maybe sleezier." Grace laughed.

"I second that," said Kristina. "Leaves nothing to be desired."

"Let's get out of here before I have to check the chick at the counter." Luz placed the lingerie back onto its rack and rolled her eyes at the salesclerk. "She's been eyeballing us since we got in here—like we're gonna steal something."

With Luz leading the way, the four of us made our way out of the store. At the sunglasses kiosk, we each tried on pairs and pairs of sunglasses—each glancing in the mirror and looking to each other for approval.

"What about these?" asked Grace.

"Too big for your face," Luz said.

"How about these?" Luz grinned as she wore a pair of mirrored sunglasses.

"Very cute," I told her. "Those are definitely you."

"Mari, try these." Kristina handed me a pair of sunglasses with green lenses. "Since you see the world through different-color lenses, I think these are perfect."

"What do you mean I see things through different-color lenses?" I asked as I placed the glasses on my face.

"You do! But I love that about you." Kristina laughed.

I took a look in the mirror.

"Those are nice," a male voice said.

Through green lenses, my eyes met Diego's. I was shocked to see him at the mall, especially since just this morning, I'd seen him handcuffed and tossed into the backseat of a police car.

"Hey," I said.

"Hey, Mari. How're you doing?" he asked.

"I'm fine."

"I heard you auditioned for at Premiere. Congratulations on getting in." Diego wore sagging jeans and a long blue T-shirt similar to the ones worn by the two boys who were with him. Diego wore a Yankees cap turned backward on his head and a blue bandanna underneath.

"Thanks," I said.

"I always knew you'd do something special with your life," he said. "Hey, Mari. About this morning..." he felt a need to explain. "Those cops are always harassing me. I can't even walk down the street in peace. They took me in for questioning...about some carjacking that took place last night. I told them I had nothing to do with it. They had to let me go."

"That's good." I didn't know what else to say.

"Hey, Luz," Diego said, glancing over at my friends who were now staring. "Grace, Kristina."

They all mumbled hellos.

"Well, anyway. I'll see you later, Mari," Diego said. "Tell Nico to hit me up on my cell phone sometime."

"Okay," I said.

He was gone just as quickly as he'd appeared. I placed the sunglasses with the green lenses back in their place.

two

Drew

LYING flat on my back and staring at the ceiling, I tossed a basketball into the air. The rubber rolled off my fingertips and into the air at least twenty times. I was stalling. Telling my dad about Premiere was weighing heavily on my mind, particularly since it'd been weeks since I'd received my letter of acceptance, yet I hadn't shared the news with him. I remembered it so well. I'd wanted to open the envelope and see what was inside, but part of me had been nervous about what I might find. To the world, I was confident, but behind closed doors I doubted myself every minute. I knew that if I hadn't made it into Premiere, I'd be forced to play basketball another year. Another year with a coach whose only concern was winning the game. It didn't matter how well we played the game—just make sure we win. Coach Austin didn't care if you had other abilities or if you had other responsibilities. Basketball was a priority. No— basketball was the only priority, according to him.

Though I loved basketball, I loved drama more. There was nothing like being onstage and transforming into someone or *something* else. It was similar to how reading a book takes you to another place—you could actually find yourself in someone else's life simply by opening the pages. Acting was like that, too. It made me feel good when I finished a scene and received applause from the audience. The applause I received from dunking a basketball couldn't really measure up.

Trying to get my father to understand that was like pulling teeth—it was hard. He couldn't see how I could possibly choose performing arts over shooting three-pointers. Particularly since basketball had been a part of my life since I was four years old. Not to mention the fact that my dad had been a starting guard for his high school and college basketball teams. And before his knee injury, there was even talk of him being drafted into the NBA. Instead he ended up playing for a European league. It's all he talked about—his high school, college and *almost-NBA* days.

It was in Europe that he met my mother, fell in love and got married. Eighteen months later, yours truly was born, and three years later my mother was gone. Veronica, the half-Italian, half-Black woman who gave birth to me, left my father to raise a three-year-old by himself. I often wondered what type of person could do that. Let my father tell it, Veronica needed to go *find herself.* I guess she was somewhere lost. At any rate, without any communication from my mother or her family, we managed, Dad and me. All I had were photos of Veronica in a nice little album she'd so thoughtfully put together for me so that I'd always remember what she looked like. I never knew my mother's family—her parents, sisters and brothers—who all lived in Europe. But with lots of help from Grandma Ernestine, my dad's mother, we did pretty well. Gram still popped in on us from time to time and made sure we had plenty to eat and fresh clean sheets on all the beds. She was obsessed with clean sheets, if you asked me. It wasn't that serious, but she thought it was—just as she thought it was important to clean underneath beds and straighten closets. What was the point? No one ever looked in people's closets or underneath their beds, and if they did, they had no business looking there in the first place.

I grabbed the envelope—the one that I'd ripped open weeks ago—from my nightstand. I read it again.

Mr. Bishop,

We would like to inform you that you have been accepted into the drama program at Manhattan's Premiere High School of Performing Arts…

I read the words over and over again, a huge grin on my face. I wanted to yell at the top of my lungs, but I didn't want to alarm Dad. I still wasn't ready to tell him my news just yet. He knew that I'd auditioned, but I'd downplayed it and made it seem as though I wasn't that interested in getting accepted and that I didn't have that much of a chance. And when he asked about whether or not I'd gotten in, I lied—told him that they hadn't made a decision yet. Besides, I was still practicing with the basketball team at my old public high school, and I was a starter for the varsity team, even though I was a merely a sophomore. My father allowed me to make my own decisions, but it was going to break his heart when he found out that I'd chosen drama over basketball.

"You hungry?" Dad appeared in my doorway.

"I could eat," I said and casually placed the letter beneath my leg.

"I fried some chicken and made some of those beanie weenie things," he said.

My father wasn't the greatest cook. In fact, we usually ate out at fast-food restaurants. The quality of food changed only when Gram came for a visit or when my dad was dating some woman who wanted to impress him with her cooking. And since Gram was getting older and traveled less these days, and my father was in between relationships, we made do with what we had—tonight's fried chicken and beanie weenies, which would become tomorrow's chicken à la surprise. My dad never professed to be a great cook or a homemaker, but he was a great father. He taught me strong values—things such as how to be a man, how to earn a living, not to expect anyone to take care of you, how to be a gentleman and to treat a woman with respect. I looked up to my dad. He was my hero.

"You seriously fried some chicken?" I asked.

"Okay, they were frozen nuggets that I defrosted in the microwave and popped into the oven for twenty minutes. You got a problem with that, kid?"

"Nope. I was just askin'." I tossed him the ball, and he caught it.

"How was practice today?"

"Um…it was…you know. Usual."

"Coach said you're looking good out there, boy."

My dad was starting to gray around his sideburns and had little speckles of gray in his mustache. Besides the gray, he looked like an older version of me. He was still physically fit, and women seemed to throw themselves at him— ugly ones, pretty ones, short ones, skinny ones. They all wanted him to commit, but Dad just wasn't the commitment type. Ever since Veronica left, all commitments went out the window.

"I'm doing all right. I'm not really feelin' it that much this year, though," I said.

"You will. It's still early. Just keep giving it your best," Dad said, then grinned and tossed the ball back to me. "Now, come on. Let's eat this gourmet meal before it gets cold."

After Dad left the doorway, I folded the letter, placed it neatly back into its envelope and stuffed it into the drawer. I grabbed my shirt from the floor, pulled it over my head and then strolled downstairs for dinner.

Dad and I ate chicken nuggets and beanie weenies while catching the latest sports updates on ESPN. Our home was the ultimate bachelor's pad—and bachelors, we were. Our living room was equipped with black leather furniture and a state-of-the-art flat-screen television, especially designed for football and basketball games, and a pool table. Our freezer was filled with TV dinners and frozen foods. In our pantry, Gatorade, Orville Redenbacher's microwavable popcorn and cans of ravioli were stacked on the shelves. The view from our Upper West Side apartment was spectacular.

Dad was in between relationships with women, and I was definitely single, although there were several girls interested. Ashley was tall, beautiful and could easily win the competition on *America's Next Top Model*. And she was intelligent. But she was too clingy. She was like a bloodhound; could find me anywhere. Like the day when I was with Mari and Preston at Manny's. Somehow she managed to just show up.

Brianna was the girl in my building. She'd had a crush on me since seventh grade, but she wasn't much of a looker. She wore a huge set of glasses until ninth grade, when she finally got contacts. Her boobs were still flat and her body was like a beanpole, and she sounded all nasally when she talked. But she was fun to hang out with. She loved sports and because her father was a retired NBA coach, he was able to get us floor seats for every Knicks game imaginable—all we had to do was ask.

Ashley was beautiful, and Brianna was fun. And I often wished I could wrap the two of them up into one person and have the best of both worlds. It was hard to find a girl in Manhattan who was pretty but not pretentious—one with Ashley's looks but Brianna's personality. I wanted a simple girl who had goals and dreams. Someone who wasn't from my neighborhood. Someone who was genuine. Someone like Mari. She was beautiful, intelligent and seemed fun. I'd found myself thinking about her long after she'd left Manny's.

"I got accepted into Premiere High," I finally admitted to Dad.

"Oh, yeah?" His eyes were glued to the television as he watched an instant replay of Terrell Owens scoring a touchdown in a preseason football game.

"Yeah, and I think I might transfer there," I said and waited for the remote control to come flying across the room and hit me in the head. When it didn't, I continued. "Um…I like acting more than basketball." I was really pushing it. "I really feel good when I'm onstage and the crowd is going crazy because I said or did something spectacular. I mean the crowd goes crazy when I dunk a basketball, too, but I don't get the same feeling. When I'm onstage, it's like having an out-of-body experience. Like I'm not even there, you know?" I was babbling.

Dad said nothing. His attention was steady on ESPN as he popped a chicken nugget into his mouth and took a big gulp from his bottle of Gatorade.

"It's not that I'm giving up on basketball." I wanted to smooth things over a bit. I felt as if I'd gotten too excited about acting. "You know, I'm still true to the game. That'll never change. Me and basketball…we're like peanut butter and jelly…cake and ice cream…beans and corn bread…"

"Are you done?" he asked.

"Um, yeah…I guess."

"Make sure you load your dishes into the dishwasher." He stood and headed out of the room. "You forgot to do it last night."

That was it. No comment on the subject at hand. Just *make sure you load the dishes into the dishwasher*? It was obvious that he had just gone through the motions when he'd given me permission to audition. I remembered how he laughed under his breath as he handed me the signed papers.

"Good luck, son," he'd stated in a joking way.

I wasn't sure if he knew that I was serious about transferring, or if he never expected me to make it in. But now, as reality hit home, he was different. Angry. Or hurt. I wasn't sure which, but it was obvious that he wasn't feeling my decision. We were sports men. Acting was for dreamers. I'd heard it a million times in my life. *Drew, just because we live in a nice neighborhood and have nice things, doesn't mean you have to be a star. Everybody's trying to be a star. Don't get caught up in the hoopla. We're Bishop men, and Bishops play ball. A good, wholesome sport that can make you a lot of money if you work it right. Stay focused.* That was Dad's favorite speech.

I wished I could tell him that I wasn't getting caught up in the hoopla. That I really was talented, and Premiere High was going to enhance my life. It wasn't about stardom and all the bright lights. I wanted to tell him all those things, but when I heard the sound of jazz filling the apartment, I knew he was lost in another place.

I loaded the dishes into the dishwasher, placed dishwashing liquid into its little compartment, started it and turned off the lights in the kitchen. On my way to my room, I peeked into the living room. My dad was reclined in his easy chair, a glass filled with ice cubes and scotch in his hand. His head was leaned against the back of the chair, his eyes closed. I opened my mouth to say something but changed my mind. I'd said all I could say.

"Hey, Drew," my dad's voice startled me. He never even opened his eyes; he'd obviously heard or smelled my presence.

I stood in the doorway of the living room. "Yeah, Dad?" I asked.

"You really wanna go to that artsy school?"

"Yeah," I said. "I do. But not without your blessing."

"What do I need to do?"

"Come with me tomorrow. There's an orientation, and parents are invited to come. You can find out what classes I'll be taking and all of that..."

"They got a basketball team?"

"Nah, Dad. No sports."

"I'd like to come...you know...check out the school and all. But I got meetings all day tomorrow."

"It's cool, Dad. There will be other stuff."

I stood there for a moment. Waited for my dad to say

something else. He was silent, and so was I. I dismissed myself.

"Good night, Dad."

"Night," he mumbled.

I made my way to my room and shut the door behind me. I had a big day ahead of me—a new school, a new challenge, a new life.

three

Marisol

ORIENTATION day was exciting. As my parents and I roamed the hallways of Premiere High School, I couldn't help smiling. I was proud to show them the dance studio, the place where I'd spend most of my time, learning and growing—the place where my dreams would come true.

"It's a nice school." Poppy smiled and smoothed my hair in the back.

"It's old and musty," said Mami, who didn't see things quite as I did.

"It's not old, Mami. It has character. And what you're smelling is not must. It's the sweat and tears of the stars who have roamed these very halls!" I said and beamed.

"You must be Marisol's parents," J.C. said. The dance instructor looked different wearing a suit rather than leotards and tights. Her hair flowed against her shoulders instead of being pulled up on top of her head. She was prettier up close, and her makeup was flawless. She grabbed my mother's hand in hers. "I'm Juliette Cruz, the dance in-

structor here at Premiere. The kids call me J.C. and probably a few other choice words."

I could tell that my mother was speechless to learn that
my dance instructor was a Latina-American woman. When
I'd spoken about the woman giving the dance class last
spring, I never revealed her race. But now, I hoped that
the small detail would work in my favor.

"Hi, Mrs. Cruz…I mean, J.C. This is my mother, Isabel
Garcia," I jumped in and said.

"Please to meet you, Senora Garcia."

"Nice to meet you, too," my mother managed.

"And this is my dad, Berto," I said.

"Senor," she said and smiled. "Very nice to meet you,
sir."

"Pleasure is mine." Poppy smiled his beautiful smile. I
could tell that he thought she was attractive; he could barely
peel his eyes from her.

"You have a very talented daughter," J.C. began. "I'm
very pleased to have her in my class. My class is demand-
ing, and not everyone makes it in. But she did. I'm sure
you're very proud that she made it into such an outstand-
ing school, too."

"Well…" My mother opened her mouth, but before she
could finish whatever negative statement she was about to
make, my father jumped in.

He gave her a sideways look and said, "We're very proud
of Marisol. We know that she's capable of achieving what-

ever she puts her mind to." Poppy gave me a reassuring smile. I was grateful for his support.

"She's got a lot of work ahead of her," said J.C., "but I have no doubt that if she puts in the hard work, she will have a great career."

"What kind of career can she really have as a dancer, Mrs. Cruz?" My mother finally got her chance to spit her venom. "A Broadway showgirl? A video vixen? Or maybe…I don't know…a dance instructor?"

Did my mother just insult this woman that she'd known for only thirty seconds? I wanted to crawl under a rock and die.

J.C. smiled anyway. "There are plenty of lucrative careers for professional dancers, senora. For instance, before I was a *lowly* dance instructor—" she giggled "—I owned one of the largest dance studios in the country, where I taught ballroom and Latin dance. I choreographed routines for several celebrities. In fact, I come from a long line of dancers. My great-grandfather danced with Fred Astaire and Gene Kelly. I ended up here, teaching dance to young people at a Manhattan performing arts school, because I wanted to settle down…start a family…" She extended her hand, showing off an engagement ring. "I'm getting married in a few months."

"Congratulations," Poppy said.

"I'm sorry if I offended you…" Mami offered.

"No apology necessary, senora," J.C. said. "I can tell

that you love your daughter very much, and you only want what's best for her."

"Yes." Mami finally smiled. "I just want her to receive a good education. One that will prepare her for college."

"Then you've enrolled her in the right place. Academics are very important here at Premiere. She'll receive a wonderful education here. Most of the classes are college-prep courses, and she must maintain a certain grade point average in order to remain here. Students do not have the luxury of slacking off. They must focus on the traditional courses as well as the arts."

"That's good to know," Poppy stated; he seemed to release a sigh of relief.

"If you'll excuse me, I need to meet some of the other parents." J.C. seemed to be very likable. I was sure that she and I would get along very well. "It was very nice meeting you both. Marisol, I'll see you bright and early in the morning."

"Okay," I said and watched as J.C. disappeared into the crowd and began to mix and mingle with the other parents.

Without notice, someone walked up from behind and whispered, "Guess who?"

I grinned after recognizing Drew's voice. My parents' smiles disappeared immediately. My father frowned, and my mother's eyebrows rose in discontent at the fact that I'd already made a friend—a male friend. They had no idea that I'd been secretly searching for him all night.

"What's up?" he asked.

"Same old, same old," I said.

"Hello, sir, I'm Drew Bishop." He held out his hand and offered my father a handshake.

Poppy was hesitant at first but eventually took Drew's hand in a firm grip.

"I'm Marisol's very strict father, Berto Garcia." My father's voice had deepened.

"Pleased to meet you, sir," Drew said, "Ma'am." He nodded toward my mother.

"Hello," she managed to say. And that was all she said.

"I take it you attend here, as well?" Poppy asked the obvious. He was trying to make conversation.

"Drew's an actor," I boasted. "He was accepted into the drama department."

"That's very nice," Poppy stated.

"Would you mind if I stole your daughter for a moment?" Drew was bold; he didn't beat around the bush.

"Only if you promise to return her," Poppy said.

"Scout's honor." Drew raised his hand in the air, as if he were a Boy Scout. He didn't waste any time grabbing my hand and pulling me into the crowd and to the other side of the room.

"Where are we going?" I asked.

"I don't know. You just looked like you needed to be rescued."

"You were absolutely right. My parents are so stuffy."

"At least they showed up," Drew said. He poured two

cups of punch and handed me one. "My dad didn't even bother."

"Don't judge him too harshly. He only wants what he thinks is best for you. Right?"

"Sure. I guess," he said. "You look nice."

I was glad that I'd opted for the red dress that made me appear to have cleavage. It also showed off my legs and hugged my rear end.

"Thanks. So do you." I was blushing. I could feel my face burning, and I knew it was probably as red as my dress.

"Your father cracked me up. 'I'm Marisol's very strict father…'" He imitated my father and then burst into laughter. "Hey, dude, I'm just trying to take your daughter to get some punch. Is that cool?"

"Shut up." I punched him in the arm. "Don't talk about my dad. Besides, you should be more afraid of my mom."

"Yeah, she was pretty chilly, too." He went into an imitation of my mother, his voice changing into a high octave. "*Hello*…and just where do you think you're going with my daughter, young man? What are your intentions for her? She's not allowed in the South Bronx, with your pants-saggin', tattoo-havin', grill-wearin' kinfolks…"

"You're sick." I laughed hard. "That was so racist."

"Exactly!" he exclaimed. "It was so racist for your mom to think that way. She didn't say those things, but I knew that's what she was thinking."

"I doubt that she was thinking that, Drew. She's old-fashioned, but she's not a racist."

"Everybody thinks that when they meet a young black guy for the first time. They think that we're all pants-sagging, good-for-nothing wastes of time," he explained. "Have you ever dated a black guy?"

"In eighth grade," I told him as I took a sip of my punch. "Eddie Anderson."

"Good ol' Eddie…" he mocked.

"What about you? You ever dated a Latin girl?"

"I know a little bit about Latin dancing." Drew disregarded my question, took my hand and started dancing a salsa dance as if there was Latin music playing.

I hung my head in embarrassment and looked around the room to see if my parents were watching. Thankfully, there was too much going on for anyone to notice. The crowd had grown and everyone was engaged in idle conversation.

"You're cute when you're embarrassed," Drew said and laughed.

"I wasn't embarrassed," I lied.

"Right…" he said. "Your face is just beet red all the time."

"You are…a very unique person," I said.

"I've been called worse," he said. "Hey, I gotta go. This place is cramping my style. I'll see you at school on Monday."

"Okay."

"Congratulations on getting in," he said and stuffed his hands into the pockets of his Diesel jeans. He looked stylish and confident in his white polo, and I could see him achieving his acting dream.

"Same to you, dude."

Drew's energy rubbed off on me. He had me wondering about him long after he was gone and longing to see him again. I wondered if his Barbie-doll–looking girlfriend knew how lucky she was to have him. He was definitely unique. Who did the salsa in the middle of a school's orientation when there was no music playing?

I watched as Drew disappeared into the crowd and then made his way out the door. I searched for my parents, who'd been cornered by the freshmen guidance counselor. I decided to go rescue them. I poured two cups of punch and headed their way.

four

Marisol

In the locker room I peeled off my street clothes as quickly as I possibly could before hopping into my leotard and tights. After stuffing my clothes into my bag, I rushed into the hallway. The halls were filled with students as I pressed my way through to my dance class. Many of them stood around chattering, practicing a dance routine, singing or rehearsing their lines to some play. Subconsciously I searched for Drew. I hoped that I'd run into him, but the chances were slim. There were too many people. Instead, I found my way to the dance studio. The bag that was slung across my shoulder held an extra pair of leotards and a pair of shorts, as well as a few spiral notebooks and a three-ring binder.

I pushed open the heavy door and every eye in the class landed on me. I was late. My alarm hadn't gone off as it should have, and I totally messed up my first day of school. Being late on the first day at a new school was not fun. The last thing you wanted to do was draw attention to yourself by walking into your first class after everyone else was there. I tried not to look at anyone and attempted to make myself inconspicuous at the back of the class.

"We're glad you could join us, Miss Garcia," said J.C. as she paced the floor. "Is this going to be your regular time of arrival?"

"Um…I'm sorry. My alarm clock didn't…um…" I couldn't even bring myself to complete the sentence.

The giggles throughout the room caused my temperature to rise. I was embarrassed.

"My class begins at 8:00 a.m. sharp. Not 8:01, and certainly not 8:15. The rules at Premiere High are different from the ones you might be used to at your regular public high school. The young men and women here are committed to their education and their craft." This was not the same J.C. who charmed my parents the other night at the orientation. No…this one was different. There was no smile, no suit and no flowing hair.

I didn't really see the need for a lecture on my first day of school. I was late—no doubt about it. But really, was it that serious? As I took a look around the room, finally making eye contact with a few students, I wanted to crawl into a corner and never resurface. Some of them still had smirks on their faces; some of them simply rolled their eyes. I was glad when J.C. finally moved on.

"We're going to begin by stretching, so if we can line up in three rows of ten."

Everyone did as J.C. instructed and arranged themselves in three rows of ten, facing the mirrored wall.

"Where did you take the subway from?" The thin girl who stood next to me began to stretch her long, lean legs.

"Sunset Park."

"Brooklyn," she stated matter-of-factly in her strong New York accent. "What station?"

"Thirty-sixth street."

"I'm in Bed-Stuy. Maybe we can kinda look out for each other. Maybe ride into the city together." She was a mixed girl, with light brown skin and long sandy-colored locks that brushed against her shoulders. Her light brown eyes were friendly.

"Thank you," I whispered. "I'm Marisol. Everyone calls me Mari."

"I'm Jasmine," she said. "Meet me in front of the cafeteria at lunchtime. We can exchange numbers and maybe grab a bite to eat together."

Before I could respond, Jasmine was lost in the stretch routine. At the end of the class, I wanted to thank her for making me feel at ease at the worst possible time, but she was nowhere to be found. I gathered my bag onto my shoulder and headed through the crowded hallway in search of my next class.

At lunchtime I headed for the cafeteria. A blond boy with a stack of flyers in his hand tapped me on the shoulder.

"You should try out for this." He handed me a flyer. "I saw your audition the other day."

I took the flyer and scanned it quickly:

DANCE AMERICA
DANCE COMPETITION:
AUDITIONS BEING HELD THIS FRIDAY
AT PREMIERE HIGH'S DANCE STUDIO
5:00 PM
DO YOU HAVE TALENT?

I'd heard about the Dance America competition. Everyone who was anyone in New York had heard about the Dance America competition. It brought people from everywhere in the country—New York, Los Angeles, Chicago—there was even a boy from Utah who made it to the finals one year. And he could dance. The girl who'd won last year's competition was last seen in a movie on television. She was talented, and just thinking about her took my confidence down a few notches.

I folded the flyer, stuck it inside my algebra book and headed for the cafeteria line. I wasn't very hungry, so I grabbed a carton of milk and an order of fries. At the public school I was able to eat lunch at a reduced rate because of my parents' income, but at Premiere High, there was no free or reduced-price lunch program. Students paid for their own lunch. There were several items to choose from each day—burgers, tacos and pizza. My parents had already warned that I would have to rely on my allowance and the cash that I'd earned babysitting for lunch. And since my allowance was only ten dollars a week, and my babysitting jobs occurred only every now and then, I was definitely on a budget.

I spotted Jasmine at a table chatting with a few girls.

"Hey, what's up?" I said as I approached the table.

"Hey, Mari. What's up, girl?" Jasmine said. "Mari, this is Bridgette, Celine and Charmaine. Divas, say hello to Mari."

"Hey, Mari," Charmaine was the first to speak.

"Love your hair," Bridgette said.

"You sing, dance or act?" asked Celine, who barely looked up from her cell phone. She was sending someone a text.

"I dance," I told her.

Finally looking up, Celine challenged, "Let me see what you got."

"Right now?"

"No, tomorrow. Are you a dancer or what? Are you scared, girl?" Celine was beautiful, with long black hair and a light brown face. Her makeup was perfect.

"No, I'm not scared." I had attitude.

"Anyone who attends Premiere High should be proud to have made it in. They're not only talented, they're confident." She stood and started moving to some imaginary music, clapping her hands and shaking her hips.

Charmaine stood next to her and they started moving in unison; a routine that they'd obviously practiced together. When they were done, they gave each other a high five, as if they'd shown me.

"You won't survive here." Celine rolled her eyes and started picking over her dry-looking turkey burger and fries.

"Leave her alone." Jasmine came to my defense. "She can actually dance her behind off. She's in my intermediate dance class."

"Groovy," Celine said sarcastically and stuffed a fry into her mouth.

"Have a seat, girl," Jasmine said. "Don't pay her any mind."

I was reluctant at first but then took a seat at the table next to Bridgette. I ate my fries in silence as the four of them chatted about everything from boys to what happened in their classes the first half of the day. Jasmine and her friends were sophomores, and this was their second year at Premiere.

"Hey, Mari." I heard a familiar voice behind me and turned to find Drew carrying an orange lunch tray.

"Hey."

"You survived orientation," he said and smiled. "I knew you would."

His smile was so beautiful and gave me comfort.

"Hey, Drew," Celine cooed. Her voice was syrupy sweet all of a sudden.

"Hey, what's up, Celine?" he asked.

"Will you buy me a slice of triple cheese at Manny's after school?" she asked and grinned.

"I'll think about it." He smiled, too.

He'd think about it? How about *no*? Buy yourself a slice!

"Are you going to Manny's after school, Mari?" He turned his attention back to me, and I was grateful.

I shrugged and looked at Jasmine. We were possibly commuting home together. So if she was going, I was going. She must've read my mind.

"I could use a slice of pepperoni," Jasmine said.

"Cool," Drew said. "I'll see you there."

After school, I followed Jasmine through the double doors of the school. She hit Play on her iPod and started bouncing to a song by Drake. Then she threw her backpack over her shoulder and pulled a package of Newport cigarettes out of her worn purse. She held a cigarette between her long fingers.

"You smoke?" she asked.

"No," I said and wished that she wouldn't, either.

Secondhand smoke was worse than her filling her own lungs with it. It didn't matter. She pulled a bright green lighter from her purse and lit the cigarette anyway.

"It won't bother you if I smoke, right?" She wasn't really interested in my response, because before I could answer she'd already taken two or three puffs while bouncing to the music. "Drake is so cute, isn't he?"

"He's okay."

"Just okay? I would date him," she said. "I saw him once. At Starbucks in Times Square. He ordered a nonfat latte!

Can you believe that? A nonfat latte. Are you serious, dude? Are you really watching your fat content?"

"Everybody's pretty health conscious these days," I said.

"Everybody but me. Give me the fat. And the calories. And the sugar. All of it! You're gonna die one day anyway."

"But you don't have to kill yourself."

"You're smart." She smiled. "You gonna audition for Dance America?"

"Thinking about, it."

"I might this year, too."

As we approached Manny's, Jasmine tossed the butt of her cigarette onto the ground and smashed it with the sole of her shoe. I loved Jasmine's free-spirited attitude, but I didn't know how much of her cigarette smoking I could take. I tried not to judge her, though.

Manny's was crowded—as usual. And finding a table was a challenge as always, but we managed to secure a booth near the window. Celine and Charmaine found us and decided to squeeze into the booth with Jasmine and me. And it wasn't long before Drew and his friend Preston pulled up chairs next to our table.

With a black straw fedora on his head, Drew stuffed a slice of pizza into his mouth. His muscles bulged from his light blue T-shirt, and a silver *D* hung from the chain around his neck. And when he got up to grab a jar of parmesan cheese from an empty table, I noticed how his jeans hung off of his behind so nicely. His six-foot-tall body had the type of frame that girls looked for in a guy. The type of frame that forced you to stand on your tippy toes when you gave him a kiss. It was hard not to stare into his light brown eyes.

"That fedora is hot." Celine giggled, snatched Drew's hat from his head and placed it on her own head. "How do I look?"

"Very sexy," Drew said. "I love a woman in a hat."

"Really?" Celine asked. "What else do you love a woman in?"

"I'll get back to you on that," Drew said, "but right now, I'm gonna grab another slice. Anybody else want something?"

Everyone declined—except Celine.

"I'll go with you. I could use another slice, too."

Could she be any more forward? Could she just throw herself at him any more than that? It was obvious that she wasn't his type. I watched as she clung to his arm all the way to the counter. Her Seven jeans hugged her slender legs, and her long black hair hung down her back. With Drew's fedora on her head, she glided next to him like a dancer. And he was enjoying the attention. I could tell by the way he brushed a piece of her hair from her eyes as they stood at the counter and ordered pizza.

"So do you go to Premiere?" Jasmine asked Preston. "I haven't seen you around there."

"No. Right now, I attend Breckinridge Academy. It's a...private school."

"Oh, yeah, the preppy, stuffy school in Manhattan where all the rich kids go," Charmaine said.

"He's a Premiere High wannabe," Drew announced as he approached the table again.

"It's true. I am a Premiere High wannabe, but trying to talk my dad into letting me audition is like speaking German to him. He doesn't understand or see the need."

"Are you talented?" Jasmine was so straightforward. She wasn't the type to beat around the bush. *Just ask it.*

"I play the violin."

"Are you any good?" asked Jasmine.

"He's great!" Drew acknowledged.

"Then why won't he let you do the performing arts thing?"

"You have to understand. I don't really have a choice in the matter. My great-grandfather attended Breckinridge. And his father. And his father's father. It's a family tradition."

"I say screw tradition if it means compromising what you love," said Jasmine.

"It's not that easy when you come from a traditional-family background," said Preston.

"Yeah, like me," I said. "My parents were reluctant, too. They don't want a career in show business for me. They seem to think that all celebrities wind up in rehab or end up destroying their lives somehow. They want me to become a doctor or lawyer."

"My father didn't take the news well about me making

it in, either," Drew admitted. "I was a basketball star at my old high school. My coach had high hopes for me. My father played semipro basketball in his former life, so...he expected the same from me. Wanted to live out his dreams through me."

"Not my parents. They don't care where I attend school." Jasmine took a long sip of her Cherry Coke. "Just as long as I go to school somewhere and it doesn't cost them any money. Things are tight for us right now. That's why I have to win this competition...Dance America."

"What's Dance America?" asked Preston.

"It's only the most popular dance competition in the nation," Charmaine said.

"Kids come from performing arts schools all over the United States," Celine said. "The competition is stiff, but I made it to the finals last year."

"You're trying out, right, Mari?" Drew asked.

"Considering it." I hadn't given it any serious thought.

"You have to bring your A game," Celine added, as if I didn't have an A game or as if I was too dumb to know what an A game was.

"You should seriously consider it," Drew added. "Who knows what might happen? You could wind up being a star!"

"I'm auditioning again." Celine smiled at Drew as if she was searching for the same encouragement that he'd given me.

When his phone played a tune, he looked at the screen

and completely ignored her comment. I couldn't help but smile.

"I would love to sit here and chitchat with you guys all day, but duty calls," Jasmine announced.

"You got a job?" Preston asked.

"Yeah, babysitting my bratty little brother while my parents go to work at New York Methodist Hospital," she said.

"Are they doctors?"

"No. My dad's a janitor, and my mom's a nurse. Like I always say, at least if he passes out from cleaning all the toilets, she'll be there to revive him." She giggled and then turned to me. "You ready, Marisol?"

"Yeah," I said and grabbed my bag from underneath the table. "Catch you guys later."

"Later," Drew said.

"See ya, ladies," said Preston, as he stood in a gentleman-like manner. It wasn't often that boys actually treated girls like ladies. He was a rare breed. "You need me to walk you guys to the subway?"

"Nah, I think we can manage, dude, but thanks for asking," said Jasmine as she pushed her way through the crowd at Manny's.

I followed. And soon we were sitting side by side on a train Brooklyn-bound. My mind began to wander to the possibilities of competing for Dance America. I knew I could dance. And I had just as much of a chance as anyone at making it into the competition. I just needed the courage to compete, and my parents' permission, of course—which was even more of a challenge than the competition itself.

As Jasmine's head bounced against the window, her mouth opened and light snores crept from her lips. I smiled, glad I'd run into her at my dance class. I gave her a nudge as we approached her station in Bedford-Stuy. She straightened in her seat, gathered herself. As she stood to exit the train, she pulled the package of cigarettes from her purse and gave me a grin.

"See you tomorrow. Bright and early. I'll text you when I get up."

"Okay."

She hopped from the train, her backpack in tow. Suddenly she was lost in the crowd. I gazed out the window. Day one started off badly, but it hadn't ended too badly at all.

five

Marisol

AS I made my way around the corner of my block, Luz, Kristina and Grace stood in front of Luz's house, stretching their necks my way. Within moments, my three friends were there, Luz grabbing my bag from my shoulder.

"How was your train ride from Manhattan?" she asked.

"It wasn't too bad. I met a new friend. Jasmine…she lives in Bed-Stuy."

"With a name like Jasmine, she's not Mexican," Grace announced, as if I didn't already know.

"No, she's not," I said.

"Well, what is she?" Grace asked.

"She's mixed."

"So how was your first day at Bourgeois High?" Luz asked.

"Oh, Luz, it was so wonderful. There were so many kids there you could barely make it through the hallways. And everyone is a dancer, musician or actor." I'd waited all day just to share my excitement with them. "I was late to my dance class this morning. My alarm clock didn't go off. That's how I met Jasmine…"

"Jasmine?" asked Kristina.

"Yeah, the girl that I rode home with on the subway."

"Oh, yeah, the mixed girl," Grace said.

"We're gonna ride into Manhattan together every morning. And she's gonna text me every morning so that I don't oversleep anymore," I said. "And you guys should see her dance. She's an awesome dancer!"

"Well, isn't that sweet?" Luz said sarcastically. She wasn't fond of anyone she thought might replace her as my best friend. "Are you gonna do my hair today or what?"

"Yeah, of course." I'd forgotten all about agreeing to do Luz's hair. I'd promised to do it as soon as I made it home from school. What I really wanted to do was lie across my bed, reminisce about my first day of school and then get a jump start on my homework. There was no room for relaxation. My grades were a priority, especially since they determined my future at Premiere.

"Where you been all day? We all got home like two hours ago," Grace said.

"All of the kids hang out at Manny's after school."

"Is this going to be an everyday thing or what?"

"Probably so. Everybody hangs out there." I grabbed my bag from Luz's shoulder and started up the stairs to my house. "Let me go inside and say hello to my parents. I'll be at your house in twenty minutes."

"Okay, Chica. Hurry up. Your mom's been talking to

my mom again—about eating together as a family and all
that stuff about bonding as a family. It's been months since
we had an official dinnertime, but thanks to Isabel Garcia,
now my mom insists that the whole family eat together
again. She thinks that's why my dad and her are having
marital problems—because we stopped eating together.
How silly is that?" Luz asked and then walked across the
street toward her house. Kristina and Grace followed.

It was no secret that my mom and Luz's mom were the
best of friends. Often, they shared ideas about raising us and
about how we acted as families. Because of their friendship,
Luz and I were raised pretty much the same—same values and same rules. Sometimes their friendship got in the
way, especially when they put their heads together about
something that affected Luz and me.

My mom stood in the kitchen, an apron tied around her
waist and her long hair pulled back into a ponytail. Isabel
Garcia gave me a bright, unexpected smile.

"Hola, bebé. ¿Cómo es hoy?" She asked how my day was
in her Spanish dialect. We were a bilingual family and used
a mixture of Spanish and English at home.

"It was okay," I said, and asked what she was cooking.
"¿Qué estás cocinando?"

"Chicken. Are you hungry?" she asked.

"Not really. I had a slice at Manny's, a pizza joint in
Manhattan."

"You went there after school?"

"All the kids do," I explained.

"According to my sources, she was hanging out with some cute girl, with curly hair and light brown eyes," my brother, Nico, said as he entered the kitchen, grabbed a chunk of papaya from the kitchen counter and popped it into his mouth, then grabbed another one. "Rode the subway with her."

"What, are you stalking me?" I asked Nico.

"I have my spies." He grinned. "So watch your back."

"You made a new friend?" Mom asked.

"Her name's Jasmine," I said to my mother.

"Can I meet her?" Nico asked. "I hear she's hot."

My brother was the spitting image of my father, with dark hair. We both had Poppy's eyes and smile. Nico was handsome, and the girls in the neighborhood usually made a fuss over him. I wasn't quite sure why. He was my brother, but I didn't see him as the sexy eye candy that my friends thought he was. Nico was somewhat shy and only recently started becoming more flirtatious with girls.

"No, she doesn't want to meet you." I snatched the papaya from Nico's fingertips and popped it into my mouth.

"How do you know she doesn't? I'm good-looking, I'm smart…"

"That's a matter of opinion," I said and headed out of the kitchen.

I took the stairs up to my room, tossed my bag across my bed and searched for a pair of sweatpants. I found the blue ones with AEROPOSTALE written across the butt in bold white letters; pulled them on. I also changed into a white AEROPOSTALE T-shirt. I pulled my long black hair into a ponytail and slipped on a pair of white flip-flops. I searched for my shampoo, conditioner and blow-dryer; tossed the stuff into a bag and headed downstairs.

"Mami, I'm going to Luz's."

Mami was at the kitchen table, wrapped up in one of her celebrity-gossip tabloids. She tried to hide it as I entered the room, but I knew that she read those things. She left them all over the house. They were filled with stories of fallen stars—celebrities who'd gotten caught up in scandals, strung out on drugs and alcohol and all sorts of things that I thought were mostly lies. But Mami believed all of the smut that she read in those magazines. It was obvious that she enjoyed reading about how stardom had led some celebrity down a road of destruction, and it was why she didn't want me to become a star. She was afraid that I'd get caught up in a glamorous Hollywood lifestyle, and before long I'd sell my soul to the devil, lose all self-esteem and get strung out on drugs. She didn't want me to end up the same as the people she read about in those magazines.

"Look at that child star, Miley Cyrus. Look what happened to her." That was always her favorite argument. "Her father just tossed her to the wolves."

I had to make her see that not all celebrities were fallen— they weren't all involved in scandals and they didn't all need rehab. Some of them actually made something of their lives and had wonderful careers. It was going to be hard to convince her, but I would if it took the rest of my life.

She walked over to the stove and stirred something in a pot. "Be back before dinner."

Dinner was ritually at six o'clock. My father usually made it home from the construction site by five-thirty, took a long shower and came straight to the dinner table, where the rest of us awaited. Since my mother worked only part-time as an elementary school teacher, she spent most of her days keeping house and preparing meals for us. It was important to my parents that we ate dinner together as a family. Around the dining room table, we prayed and then shared food and the details of our day. For Nico and me, being late was punishable, so we made it a point of making it on time every single day. My parents taught us that our time together as a family should be a priority, and nothing was more important.

As I made my way across the street, Nico was already in a game of basketball with Alejandro, Fernando and a few boys from another neighborhood.

"Hey, Mari," Fernando said and grinned. He'd had a crush on me since the beginning of time. Although he was cute, he was more like a brother to me. He had spent too many nights at my house with Nico. I could never date him.

"*Hola,* Fernando," I said.

"What's it like at that artsy school?" he asked.

"Are you gonna start acting like you're better than all of us now?" asked Alejandro.

"I'll always be the same Mari."

"You were always a little stuck-up. You're gonna continue to be that girl?" Alejandro asked with a grin. He had always been a thorn in my side.

"Leave her alone, and take the ball out, man." Nico tossed Alejandro the ball.

"It was nice to see you, Mari," Fernando said with dreamy eyes. "You look as beautiful as ever."

"Spell *beautiful,* stupid," said Alejandro as he threw the ball at Fernando, slamming it into his chest.

Soon they were all lost in the game. I stepped onto Luz's porch, rang the doorbell.

"What took you so long?" Luz asked and yanked me inside before I could answer.

The smell of something burning hit me in the nose as we walked past the kitchen. Luz's mom was fanning smoke with a dish towel.

"*Hola,* Mrs. Hernandez."

"*Hola, Mari. ¿Cómo estás?*" Luz's mom asked how I was doing as she opened the back door and let the smoke out.

"*Estoy, bien.*" I told her that I was okay.

Luz quickly ushered me upstairs to her room, for fear that her mother might ask us to help in the kitchen. Grace was reclined on Luz's bed, flipping through a Latina teen magazine. Demi Lovato graced the cover. Kristina was sitting at the foot of the bed, snacking on potato chips.

"She can't cook!" Luz exclaimed after we were behind her closed bedroom door. "My dad is the cook in the family. I don't even know why she insists on trying. She's burning things up, and then she'll insist that we all sit at the table together and eat it."

"Give her a break. At least she's trying." I felt sorry for Mrs. Hernandez.

"Your mother did this to me!" Luz exclaimed. "Talking about how you guys eat dinner around the freaking table every day and discuss your problems. Now my mom wants us to do it again! Nobody wants to eat together. And I don't care how anybody's day went. I'd much rather just grab a bowl of Froot Loops and eat it in my room."

I laughed.

"Where's my blue eye shadow!" Anarosa, Luz's younger sister, burst through the door.

"I didn't have it," Luz snapped.

"Well, it's not where I left it, and I want it back now!" Anarosa demanded.

It was always lively at Luz's house. She argued a lot with her younger sister, and their parents argued a lot with each other, too. If they weren't devout Catholics, they probably would've divorced years ago. When they were in public, they pretended to be this normal, happy family. But behind closed doors, they were far from normal. Mr. and Mrs. Hernandez believed that their daughters were good, wholesome teenagers who could do no wrong. But the truth was, Anarosa was the girl whom the football team and basketball team had tossed around since she was twelve. If Carlos Hernandez knew that his baby girl climbed out of her bedroom window on a regular basis, he'd probably have a heart attack and die. And Luz—who was a tomboy—totally transformed into a different person when her parents weren't around. She loved to challenge authority and take the wrong kinds of risks that the rest of us weren't comfortable with taking. It was Luz who'd convinced us all to take the subway into the Bronx when we were ten years old. We weren't even allowed to leave our neighborhood, let alone ride the subway into another borough.

"Get out of my room," Luz commanded. "You look like a natural-born *puta* when you wear that stuff on your eyes."

"You're a whore!" Anarosa returned the sentiment, and then stormed out of Luz's room, slamming the door behind her.

"Puta!" Luz yelled. "Come on, Mari, let's get started before Senora Loca starts calling me for dinner."

I washed Luz's hair in their bathtub, and then blow-dried and curled it. When I was done, she checked it out in the mirror.

"You missed this part," she said, holding on to a small piece of hair that I'd missed.

"You're so hard to please, Luz," I said and grabbed the curling iron to finish her hair.

"You wouldn't leave your hair undone, Chica. So don't leave mine that way," she said.

"Whatever."

"Guess what?" She changed the subject. "Pedro Vargas is walking me to class tomorrow."

"What?" I was surprised. Luz never gave any boy the time of day. Several boys liked her. Why wouldn't they? She was gorgeous: a perfect size seven, long legs, shoulder-length brown hair and beautiful olive-colored skin. "Nerdy Pedro?"

"He's not so nerdy this year. You should see him, Mari. He grew a few inches taller over the summer. And it really looks like he's been working out."

"Pedro Vargas has been working out?" I couldn't help but laugh. Grace laughed, too.

"Okay, laugh, you two. But he's different. He's not the same Pedro that you remember," she said. "We were in American history class this morning and he asked me if I had an extra pencil. As I handed him the pencil, I looked into those eyes. I don't know…I never knew that his eyes were so beautiful until then."

It was weird hearing my best friend talk about a boy this way. She usually described boys as being stupid, brainless or ugly. Never in a romantic sense. And definitely not Pedro Vargas, who was shorter than average and wore thick glasses. I couldn't understand how she could've possibly seen his eyes through those bifocals.

"Remember those thick glasses he used to wear?" she asked. "Well, he got contacts."

"Wow" is all I could say. "Well, let's get your hair done right then, girlfriend."

"That's what I said in the beginning," she said with a smile. "So, any cuties at your school, Mari?"

"I haven't really been looking. I mean…I don't know. There's this one guy that I bumped into at the auditions. Drew Bishop. He's a drama major. Good-looking," I told her. I was surprised at my own assessment of Drew.

"You like him, don't you?" Luz asked and grinned.

"He's okay," I lied.

"He's okay? Seriously? Come on, Chica, it's me…Luz. Don't lie to me!"

"Okay, I like him. But he doesn't know it," I said. "Besides, I'm sure he has a girlfriend. She showed up at Manny's one day. She's tall and beautiful…"

"So?"

"And then there's this girl, Celine."

"Who's Celine?"

"She's a snob…a very beautiful snob, who also likes Drew."

"Sounds like he's up for grabs," Grace said.

"I'm not interested," I said as I finished styling Luz's hair. "I'm more interested in Dance America."

"What's that?" Luz asked.

"It's that dance competition," Grace interjected. "Kids from all over the country compete."

"Oh, yeah, I think I heard something about that last year. The girl who won got to be in a movie or something," said Luz.

"I'm thinking about trying out." I smiled, looking for Luz's approval.

"Your parents won't let you."

"They might."

"Come on, Mari. They didn't even want you to audition at Premiere."

"Well, they don't have to know…not initially. If I'm selected, they'll be so excited for me that they won't be able to say no."

"You're dreaming," Luz said.

"You should try out, too, Luz. We could do it together."

"Who? No, not me. I like dancing, but I'm not as good as some of the people who will be competing."

"Luz, you're one of the best dancers I know. You have to try out! You have to," I begged. "If you do it, I'll do it. And our parents won't even have to know."

"Where are these auditions held?" she asked.

"At my school."

"I don't know, Mari."

"Come on. This is an opportunity of a lifetime, Luz. This is our chance."

Grace's head was bouncing back and forth between us. Luz took a look at herself in the mirror. She must've been satisfied with her hair, because she didn't complain anymore.

"Okay," she said. "I'll audition with you."

"Yes!" I exclaimed.

"I don't know why I let you talk me into these things," she said and then opened her closet and started looking for an outfit for school. "What do you think of these jeans with this top?"

"Cute," I told her. "I gotta go. It's almost six o'clock, and I have to be home for dinner."

"We gotta come up with a routine for this…this…Dance America thing."

"We'll start tomorrow," I said and started gathering my hair products. "As soon I get home from school."

"After pizza at Manny's, of course," she said sarcastically.

"Of course," I grinned and then gave my best friend a hug. "See you tomorrow."

"Okay, Chica," she said and smiled. "Why don't you sneak me some dinner from your house later. I'm sure I'll still be hungry. Besides, your mom's a much better cook."

"You're sick."

"I'm honest."

"Bye, Gracie," I said.

"See ya, Mari."

I pulled Luz's bedroom door shut behind me; jogged down the stairs and out the front door. The thought of us auditioning for Dance America made me want to skip all the way home. And I did.

SIX

Drew

MY alarm went off and Hot 97 disc jockey Cipha Sound's voice shook me out of my sleep. When I heard a Timbaland song, I turned the radio up as loud as it would go and rolled out of bed, wearing a pair of boxers but no shirt. I went into the bathroom, splashed water onto my face and turned on the shower. As I stepped into the shower, I started rehearsing my lines for the school's production of *A Raisin in the Sun*. Today, I would be auditioning for the role of Walter Lee Younger. It was the role that P. Diddy portrayed in the modern version of the play. The old version premiered in 1959. It was a Broadway play, and the role of Walter Lee Younger was played by Sidney Poitier. I had gone to Blockbuster and rented the 1961 version of the film, which also starred Sidney Poitier. For a few days, I studied my scenes in the hopes I could get my lines, tight as Mr. Poitier's. He was so smooth. And if I landed the role, the production would take place in an off-off-Broadway stage in the city. It was that thought that made it all worthwhile.

Freshly dressed, and with cologne dabbed on my neck,

I grabbed my keys from the kitchen bar and headed for the garage. I hopped into my car. I could've walked the twelve blocks from our apartment to school, but occasionally I liked to take my car out for a spin. I knew that my father would probably flip a lid if he found out, but what he didn't know wouldn't hurt him. I let the top down just to catch a little bit of the New York City morning breeze. I popped in a Keri Hilson CD and tried to visualize her beautiful body moving to the music. She was exactly what I needed first thing in the morning. Keri was someone of interest to me. Besides writing songs for people like Britney Spears, Ludacris and Usher, she also attended Oxford University, where she majored in theater. I was somewhat of a songwriter; I had spiral notebooks filled with songs that I'd written. I used songwriting as a way of expressing my feelings. Whether I had a good day or a bad one, I could write a song about it. We had so much in common—Keri and me. All she had to do was recognize that I was alive.

I bounced to the music as I sat in bumper-to-bumper traffic on Fifth Avenue. The drive should've taken only a few minutes, but during New York's rush-hour traffic, it was the worst drive ever. But I took it in stride; I tried to make the best of each day, no matter the challenge. It wasn't always easy, but at least I tried. Some days I didn't do so well. The cab driver in the car next to mine blew his horn and shouted profanity to someone in the car in front of him. Loud horns sounded throughout the city as people made their way to wherever their destination was. The car in front of me stalled, and just as I put my blinker on to go around him, cars began to pile up in the lane next to mine. It seemed there was no way out, and if traffic didn't start moving soon, I'd be late for school.

Being late for drama class was unacceptable. Harold Winters, my instructor, made it very clear that attendance and grades determined which roles you received in certain productions. The slackers almost always ended up being understudies. I wasn't interested in being anyone's understudy. I wanted the lead. I took acting seriously, especially since I had something to prove to my father. There was no time for half stepping. I had to make him believe that his only son hadn't become soft. That acting didn't make me any less of a man. In fact, it brought out the best in me. I could act just as well—maybe even better—than I could play basketball. I needed for him to respect my choice.

Finally pulling into the school's parking lot, I stopped at the security gate and let my window down.

"Where's your parking pass?" the heavy female security guard asked.

"Um…I…" I pretended to search for it in my wallet.

"You won't find it in your wallet. It's too big to fit in there. It goes on the dash of your car." Her dark brown face frowned at me. She looked as if she might actually be pretty if she took the time to apply a little makeup, curl her hair and possibly lose a few pounds.

"I must've forgotten to get it." I gave her that award-winning smile that usually charmed women. "It's probably at the house…"

"Well, I would suggest you go back to *the house* and get it," she said, "'cause you can't park here without it."

Did she have to be so mean? I wondered what she would look like if she smiled. She obviously didn't know who I was. My father was a local celebrity—a sportscaster for a major New York radio station. He had his own show between the hours of six and eight in the morning, Monday through Friday. And he'd made guest appearances on ESPN's *SportsCenter*. He'd interviewed Eddy Curry, Amar'e Stoudemire and other great Knicks basketball players over the years.

"I know…you probably don't know who I am. I am the son of New York's very own morning sportscaster, Big 'D' Bishop. If you look at the tag on the front of the car, it says BISHOP2. This one's mine. He drives the Lexus… the lucky dog. He's BISHOP1…"

She took a look at the tag on the front of the car, as if she was really considering what I'd just said.

"Does your father also attend Premiere High School?"

"No, ma'am."

"Then why do I care what car he drives and what his tag says?" She frowned again. "Now, what I need for you to do is turn this little car around…go back home and find your parking pass."

"Can you let me go just this one time?"

"No can do," she stated. "Now, if you don't mind...there are others behind you."

I took a glance into my rearview mirror, and sure enough, there were four cars behind me waiting to get into the parking lot. They started blowing their horns. I did just as the security officer asked me to do and turned the car around. I didn't have a parking pass at the house. There was no need for one. Actually, there was no need for me to drive to school at all. I circled the block a few times, in search of a parking meter; somewhere I could park for a few hours until I figured something else out. I finally found an empty space and parallel-parked in between two cars. I stepped out of the car and dug deep into my pockets in search of spare change. I filled the meter with enough change for three hours—enough time to make it to my audition and to make it back outside around lunchtime to pump more change into it. I grabbed my backpack from the backseat and sprinted toward the school.

Winters raised an eyebrow as I entered the room. He glanced at his watch, and I knew he was not happy that I'd walked into his class ten minutes late. Especially after his thirty-minute lecture on the first day of school regarding attendance and tardiness. I found a seat in the third row and watched as Jason Michaels auditioned for my role.

"Yeah. You see, this little liquor store we got in mind cost seventy-five thousand, and we figured the initial investment on the place be 'bout thirty thousand, see," Jason said. He actually sounded pretty good as he continued to read the lines of Walter Lee Younger. "That be ten thousand each. 'Course, there's a couple of hundred you got to pay so's you don't spend your life just waiting for them clowns to let your license get approved..."

The entire class applauded as he took a bow and stepped down from the stage.

"Anyone else for the role of Walter Lee Younger?" Winters asked in his Southern drawl. Even though he'd been a New Yorker for a several years, Mr. Winters never lost his Mississippi accent. On the first day of school, he boasted about his days at Julliard, where he studied drama. Julliard was definitely a school that I had my eye on for college.

I stood and headed for the stage.

"Where are your notes, Mr. Bishop?" Winters asked.

"I don't need any. I memorized my lines," I said and then hopped onto the stage. I stood at center stage and cleared my throat. "Anybody who talks to me has got to be a good-for-nothing loudmouth, ain't he? And what you know about who is just a good-for-nothing loudmouth? Charlie Atkins was just a 'good-for-nothing loudmouth,' too, wasn't he! When he wanted me to go in the dry-cleaning business with him. And now—he's grossing a hundred thousand a year. A hundred thousand dollars a year! You still call *him* a loudmouth!"

After reciting the entire scene, I took a bow and exited the stage. Winters wrote some notes down as I went back to my seat.

"Thank you, Mr. Bishop," Winters said. "Now for the role of Mama."

"Can I go first?" asked the beautiful caramel-colored girl who I'd noticed on the first day of school. She had soft features and bright eyes. Not to mention a dimple in her chin when she smiled. She wore tight jeans and a shirt that hugged her breasts. I couldn't imagine her transforming into the role of an old woman, but anything was possible in the theater.

"Very well, Miss Bell," Winters stated.

She slipped out of her seat and took the stage. Her long brown hair was pulled into a ponytail. She stood there for a moment with her head hung, and when she raised it, she had transformed into Mama.

"Child, when do you think is the time to love somebody the most? When they done good and made things easy for everybody? Well then, you ain't through learning—because that ain't the time at all. It's when he's at his lowest and can't believe in hisself 'cause the world done whipped him so!" Without any notes, her strong New York accent had become a Southern drawl, like Winters's. "When you starts measuring somebody, measure him right, child, measure him right. Make sure you take into account what hills and valleys he come through before he got wherever he is."

I was impressed. She was a female version of me. Good-looking and talented. Both those things wrapped up into one made for a dangerous combination. Nonetheless, I had to make her acquaintance. After class, I rushed her.

"You're definitely the right choice for the role of Mama," I told her.

She smiled and the entire room lit up. "And you were a pretty good Walter yourself."

"Winters called you Miss Bell, but I didn't catch your first name."

"Asha."

"Asha Bell, I'm Drew...Drew Bishop."

"It's nice to meet you, Drew Bishop." She gathered her things; stuffed them into her backpack.

"How long have you been acting?" I asked. I couldn't pry myself away.

"Since I was like five years old. What about you?"

"About that long." I was just about to ask her what her after-school plans were.

"Okay, you ready?" asked Jason Michaels as he took Asha's backpack from her shoulder.

"Yeah, I'm ready," she said. "It was nice meeting you, Drew."

"Hey, bro. Your audition was pretty good. I wish you luck," Jason said and then grabbed his woman around her waist.

"Thanks, same to you," I lied. I didn't want to wish him luck. I wanted the role of Walter Lee Younger more than anything, and I hoped Jason's acting abilities hadn't overshadowed mine. And on top of it, he had the pretty girl. As Jason grabbed Asha by the hand, I watched as they exited the theater. He didn't need any more luck than he already had.

I rushed outside to pump more change into the meter where my car was parked. I turned the corner just in time to find a meter maid slapping a ticket onto my windshield.

"Hey!" I yelled. "Wait a minute! I was about to feed the meter."

"Sorry." The disgruntled red-haired man with a five o'clock shadow frowned and moved on to the next car.

"Can you take this back and let me put change in the meter? Just this once?"

"No can do. The meter ran out, dude."

"You don't understand. If my father finds out that I drove this car to school, and got a parking ticket…"

It was worthless trying to explain. I snatched the ticket from the windshield, looked at it.

"You wouldn't happen to have change, would you?" I asked, not really expecting a serious response.

Red hair rolled his eyes. I looked around, searching for someplace I could get change. As I stepped inside a corner store, I knew that I would be late to my next class. Driving had turned out to be more trouble than it was worth.

seven

Marisol

AS the train came to a screeching halt at the Thirty-sixth Street station, I nudged Jasmine. She'd already started to doze before we'd left Manhattan. She was tired most afternoons because her mornings began so early. She had to care for her younger brother before school every day—making sure he was dressed and fed before escorting him to day care, which was two train stops in the opposite direction. Her evenings were spent babysitting him; reading to him before feeding him and making sure he bathed before bedtime. And after all of that, she stayed up half the night doing her own homework. And still found time every morning to send me a wake-up text and save me a seat on the train. That was impressive.

I liked her and was glad that we were becoming friends. And since her mother finally had a day off, she had given Jasmine permission to follow me home to Sunset Park, so that we could work on a routine for Dance America. The first few rounds were group rounds, and what better three dancers to form a group than Jasmine, Luz and me? We were the best three dancers I knew. I couldn't wait to introduce Jasmine to Luz. I'd rambled on about Jasmine to Luz, and about Luz to Jasmine. I figured it was time that each of them put a face with a name.

Jasmine and I hopped off the train at Thirty-sixth Street and took the escalator up to the street level. We stopped at the Mexican ice cream vendor on the corner and I bought Jasmine a paleta, which is a Mexican ice pop, before heading down The Block. Luz, Kristina and Grace were in their usual spot on Luz's stoop as we came around the corner. They rushed over when they saw me.

"Hey, Mari," Grace said and grabbed my paleta; took a huge bite of it. "How was school?"

"It was fine," I said and snatched the paleta back.

"I bet you're Jasmine," said Kristina. "We've heard a lot about you."

"Don't believe everything you hear," Jasmine said with a grin.

"Jasmine, meet Grace, Kristina and Luz. Everybody, this is Jasmine."

"Nice to finally meet you." Grace gave a warm, sincere smile.

Grace was the peacemaker in our group. She hated conflict and she never met a stranger. She had a knack for making people feel at home. She believed that everyone had a good heart; it was just life's circumstances that altered who they were. She believed that murderers and rapists were ultimately good people; just victims of circumstance. Kristina

was the smart one. She aced every test and had perfect attendance since the first grade. She took life way too seriously. We had to force her to let her hair down—have fun.
Luz and I were most alike. We had a little bit of all those
characteristics all wrapped up into one. Except Luz was a
little more fragile; insecure.

"Good to finally meet you, Jasmine," said Kristina.

Luz said nothing at first. Just observed the introductions.
"I thought we were dancing today," she finally said.

"We are. At my house, as soon as I change," I announced
and headed toward my house. Jasmine followed. I looked
at Luz. "You coming or what?"

"Yeah, I'm coming."

Mami sat at the kitchen table sipping a cup of hot tea.

"Hola, bebé," she said and then asked me how was school.
"¿Cómo fue la escuela?"

"It was fine," I told her. "Mami, I want you to meet my
friend Jasmine from school. Jasmine, meet my mother, Isabel Garcia."

"Hi," Jasmine said.

"Pleased to meet you, Jasmine," Mami said. "Are you a
dancer or an actress?"

"I dance."

"She's in my dance class, Mami. And she's a very good
dancer," I said.

"Hi, Mrs. Garcia," said Luz, Kristina and Grace in
unison.

"Hello, girls," Mami said and smiled. "Sit down and have some sopaipillas."

"No, Mami, we can't. We've got work to do," I interjected and then tried to usher my friends out of the kitchen.

"I want sopaipillas," Grace whined and pushed her way back to the kitchen.

"So do I," said Kristina.

"Me three," Luz said.

The three of them took seats at the kitchen table and dug into the plate at the center of table filled with the Mexican dessert.

"What's a sopaipilla?" Jasmine asked as she stood in the doorway.

"It's sort of like a Mexican doughnut," I explained, "something that will definitely put pounds on your hips. We are dancers. We can't afford the extra weight."

"Here, try one." Grace handed one to Jasmine.

Jasmine stuffed the puff pastry into her mouth. "I think I'll take my chances."

"Let me get you all some milk," Mami said and headed for the refrigerator.

"I'm gonna go change into something more comfortable," I announced. With my backpack flung across my shoulder, I headed upstairs to my room to change clothes.

A CD player rested on the back patio. I popped in Jasmine's CD, and Willow Smith started singing about whipping her hair back and forth. Jasmine started moving to the music; a routine she'd obviously learned from the video. I followed her lead. It was a fun song and we bounced to the music as we both whipped our hair back and forth to the music. Grace and Kristina joined in.

Luz stood by, her arms folded across her chest, a frown on her face. "I don't like that song. Let's do something else."

"I like it," I told her.

"What do you mean, Luz?" Grace asked. "That song is hot!"

"On fire!" Kristina exclaimed.

"Willow Smith is like a…child…" said Luz. "It's a kiddie song."

"A very hot kiddie song," Jasmine said and then gave me a high five.

We continued to move to the music. Soon, Luz ended the CD, took it out of the player and set it on top. She popped in a different CD—an upbeat song by Justin Bieber.

"Seriously, Luz?" I asked. "How rude was that?"

"Now this song is hot!" she proclaimed and then started moving her body to the music, "and Justin is just so cute!"

"You'll have to excuse her," I told Jasmine.

"No sweat. I like JB," she said with a smile, "and he is cute."

The two of them—Luz and Jasmine—danced energetically. At first it was as if they were challenging each other to see who moved better. They began to make up routines—separate routines, but both very original. They were both very talented, and confident. I watched and admired as my two friends displayed their talent in my backyard. Grace, Kristina and I swayed from side to side and clapped our hands to the beat as we looked on.

When the song ended, I restarted it. "Both of you are great dancers. Now let's put those moves together and come up with one routine."

"That was so hot!" said Grace.

"Okay, girls." I grabbed them both by the hand. "From the top."

The three of us danced until we had successfully come up with a routine—or at least part of one. Before long, Luz had let her guard down just enough to share some moves with Jasmine, and Jasmine was more than willing to teach us what she knew. Soon we had the makings of a successful dance routine that we could all be proud of.

"The competition for Dance America will be stiff. We have to be original," I reminded them.

"Absolutely," Jasmine agreed.

"You guys need a name for your group," Grace said, and it dawned on me that in less than an hour, Jasmine, Luz and I had officially become *a group*.

"Yeah, you can't audition for Dance America without a name," said Kristina.

"They're right, you know. We do need a name," I said.

"Dance Divas," announced Kristina.

"No, that's dumb," Luz said, shooting it down. "It's not even original. Everyone calls themselves a diva nowadays."

"She's right," I agreed, "the word is overused."

"How about Premiere Princesses," Jasmine exclaimed.

"I don't attend Premiere," Luz stated with attitude. "That won't work."

"I got it," I announced. "We don't all attend Premiere, but we're all from Brooklyn. And we're all beautiful. How about Brooklyn Bellezas!"

"What's that mean?" Jasmine asked.

"Brooklyn beauties!" Grace said and grinned. "I'm loving it!"

"It's perfect," said Kristina.

"It's okay," Luz said.

"I like it," Jasmine said and then grabbed her backpack and pulled out a package of cigarettes. "Mind if I smoke?"

"Not a good idea," I said. "My mother is right on the other side of that wall. And besides, secondhand smoke is worse than the stuff you're putting into your own lungs."

"You smoke?" asked Grace.

"Yes," Jasmine stated.

"Why?" Kristina asked. She really seemed to want an answer. "You're so talented. It seems like smoking would damage your lungs and stop you from doing your best at dancing."

"It stops me from having a nicotine fit," Jasmine said with a smile. "I have to get going anyway. It's getting late."

"Can you come back tomorrow after school?" I asked, anxious for us to prepare for auditions.

"I gotta pick up my brother tomorrow. And I'm not sure when my mother will have another day off."

"Can you bring him here after you pick him up?"

"Now that's an idea," Jasmine said. "You sure it's okay with your folks if I bring him over? He's a terror."

"I'm sure they won't mind," I said.

"Okay, then we'll come over tomorrow after school," said Jasmine as she headed toward the gate.

"Wait a minute and we'll walk you to the subway station," I told her. "Let me just tell my mom where I'm going."

"Cool."

Grace, Kristina and I walked Jasmine to the subway. Luz stayed behind; claimed she had something to do for her mother. She was jealous of Jasmine. I could tell. But she didn't have reason to be. The friendship that she and I shared could never be replaced, but she had to know that I would meet new friends. I was attending a new school, with new adventures every day. And I was loving every minute of it.

eight

Drew

I exhaled after I pulled into the garage and found that my father's SUV wasn't parked in its usual place. It wasn't often that I drove my car to school. In fact, it was my father's rule that I take the Mercedes out for a spin only on weekends, and only with permission. Occasionally I broke the rules and drove Delilah to school. *Delilah*. She was my candy-apple-red birthday present when I turned sixteen. With a drop-top and a set of nice wheels, Delilah had become my prize possession. Only I didn't get to spend much time with her. She spent more time parked in our garage than she did on the streets of New York City. That was the downfall of living in a city like this—one where it was ludicrous to drive around when it made more sense to walk, grab a cab or ride the subway. What was the point in having a vehicle that you couldn't drive? Which is why I broke the rules occasionally.

Driving her to school was like heaven. Especially at my old public school, where girls went crazy over guys who owned a set of wheels. At my old school, everyone knew me. I was popular and famous—well, my dad was famous. But everyone knew that I was the son of a former semipro ballplayer and a sportscaster, and they treated me as such. There wasn't anyone who didn't know my name. However, my experience with driving Delilah to Premiere wasn't quite what I expected. There was no hype, and the parking attendant didn't even know who I was. I had to park on the street, which was dangerous. And I received a parking ticket from a disgruntled meter maid.

At my old school, I was a basketball star. I scored more points in a single game than most of my teammates scored all year. The coaches let me have my way on the court. I called the shots. At Premiere, I was nobody. I had talent and a love for the stage, but nothing more. Building a reputation all over again wasn't going to be easy, but I was up for the challenge. I needed to follow my dreams.

I pulled the Mercedes into our apartment's parking garage, lifted the top and shut off the engine. I sat there for a moment, thinking about the events of the day; especially my audition, wondering if I'd be considered for the role. There were so many talented actors in my class, some who'd been acting since preschool. My acting career consisted of the Christmas pageant at my old elementary school in sixth grade and the Easter play at Gram's Holy Ghost church in Jamaica, Queens, where she lived. It wasn't until the production of *A Christmas Carol* last year that I realized I had talent. It was then that I'd decided to pursue my acting career.

I still remember heading to the locker room during half-time at one of the biggest games of the year. I'd scored twenty-one points in the first half of the game. I was on fire! But I remember thinking that I wasn't feeling basket-ball much anymore. And it hit me that night as I jogged through the hallway of our school, and into the locker room—a towel flung across my shoulder and a bottle of Gatorade in my hand. As Coach Austin laid out his strat-egy for the second half of the game, I was dazed—in la-la land. I wanted to tell him that night that I was thinking about transferring to another school, but I didn't want to ruin the rest of the game for him or my teammates—or for my father who was sitting in the stands wearing a silver-and-blue jersey and yelling every time the officials made a bad call. I couldn't bring myself to do that to them that night. But I had a plan.

After a brief conversation with my literary arts teacher, Miss Claiborne, who encouraged me to "do something with my acting," I couldn't wait to find out more about Premiere High School's drama program. I skipped school the next day and walked the twelve blocks to the perform-ing arts school in the heart of Manhattan. I snuck in with a group of students and headed straight for the theater. With a baseball cap pulled down on my head, I took a seat in the back. Hidden by the darkness of the theater, I watched as students rehearsed lines for Shakespeare's *Romeo and Juliet*. At that moment, I knew that I belonged there.

"I have to audition for that school," I told Preston, my best friend since fourth grade.

Although we attended separate schools, Preston and I grew up together. Our fathers had been good friends and associates for a long time. I'd spent many weekends at Preston's mansion in New Jersey, where I'd learned horseback riding and how to play a round of golf. We ate lunch by ourselves at his father's country club when we were merely ten years old. When we were both twelve, Preston's father sent us to a real Knicks game in the family's Bentley. Although his nanny tagged along as our chaperone, we still had a great time.

Preston was an exceptional violinist. His love for music started when we were small boys. He'd taken private lessons and learned how to play classical music. However, when he visited our Manhattan apartment, he brought his violin and spent the evening mimicking the sounds and rhythms that he heard on the BET music videos. I didn't live in a mansion, but at our house, Preston was able to relax and be free. He didn't have to worry about the pressures of being rich. At my house we ate chicken nuggets, drank red Kool-Aid and watched ESPN and MTV. In my room, he slept in the top bunk and threw kernels of popcorn at me from above. He loved my house, and I loved his. Unlike him, I thought it was cool being rich. Although my father was somewhat wealthy, we didn't live as Preston's family did. Preston enjoyed the simple life that I had. Sometimes I wished we could switch places—if only for a week.

Preston wanted to attend Premiere High—a place where he could be free with his violin and play the type of music that he enjoyed, instead of the stuffy classical music that he learned during his private lessons. However, his father would never allow him to attend a school like Premiere. Breckinridge Academy was where his father attended high school; his grandfather and his great-grandfather also went there. His choices were slim. I often joked that Preston's father was such a busy man, he would never know if Preston were to transfer to another school. He would laugh and then throw a pillow at me.

"Shut up, Bishop," he'd say.

"No, seriously. How often do you see your dad anyway... once a week...once a month?"

"He travels a lot," Preston would say, "but he left his spies in charge. Well, one spy...the nanny, Sydney."

"She's cute," I would tease. "I could keep her distracted for you."

"You're a dreamer." He called me that all the time.

I stepped out of Delilah, grabbed my book bag from the backseat and hit the power locks. As I strolled through the parking lot, I heard the screech of tires burning rubber through the parking garage. Preston whipped his white sports car around the corner, almost running me down. He rolled the window down and gave me a wide grin.

"What's up, man?" he asked.

"Why you driving through my parking garage like a maniac?" I asked.

"I'm having a great day, my friend!" he exclaimed.

"What makes it so great?"

Instead of answering, he rolled his window up, whipped into an available parking space, stepped out of the car and raced toward me.

"We're going to a basketball game tonight," he announced.

"What game?"

"Breckinridge Academy meets…guess who…?"

"Who?"

"Your old high school!" he exclaimed.

"Are you kidding? That can't be. Private schools don't play public schools. They're in a totally different league."

"Your old coach got together with our coach and put together a scrimmage."

"Really?" I asked.

"Really," he said. "Now, I would suggest you go throw that old book bag in your room. Put on some nicer clothes. Something not so corny." He laughed.

I looked down at my argyle sweater vest and slim jeans. "No can do," I said.

"Okay, fine. Keep on the corny clothes, but come on so we don't miss the tip-off. That's my favorite part of the game," he said.

"No, I'm saying I can't go."

"Why?"

"I can't go back there. It's too soon. The wounds of my leaving haven't healed yet. I haven't seen my old coach since I broke the news to him. It would be too awkward."

"You don't have to see him," Preston said. "There will be hundreds of students in the stands. No one will even notice you."

"Are you kidding? I was voted last year's homecoming king. I was the LeBron James of the school's basketball team," I bragged. "Do you know that I never completed one homework assignment last school year?"

"That's not anything to be proud of."

"I had a girl for every subject, and they insisted on doing my homework for me. Needless to say, I aced all of my classes."

"You're a vain one, aren't you?"

"I'm not vain, just confident," I explained. "Besides, I'm not so popular anymore. Not at Premiere. When I walk through the doors there, I'm just an ordinary kid."

"Give it time, dude. As soon as you land a major role, you'll have the babes kissing your feet again," Preston said and smiled. "But for now, we got a game to go to. And I'm not taking no for an answer."

"Okay, man. Let me go change shirts. I got ketchup on my sweater at lunchtime," I said. "And by the way, did I tell you that I got a parking ticket today?"

He followed me into our apartment building, where I called for an elevator. We took it to the eighth floor.

"You didn't drive Delilah to school."

"I did."

"Your dad know?"

"Of course not," I said. "He'll never know."

After changing shirts, Preston and I headed to my former high school for the basketball game of the century. Stuffy old Breckinridge had been undefeated for the past two years. It would definitely be an interesting game.

In the stands of my old stomping grounds, I watched the game through dark shades and a baseball cap pulled down low on my head. We missed tip-off, but the first quarter of the game was filled with excitement. Breckinridge was ahead by two points, and one of its players was at the free throw line. I watched as Coach Austin paced back and forth across the buffed floor, that usual wrinkle in between his eyes. He seemed stressed out all the time; too stressed to be coaching a bunch of knuckleheaded teenagers. Breckinridge's center, a tall guy with blond hair, sank both free throws into the basket, placing his team ahead by four points.

"Drew Bishop. Is that you?" asked the girl wearing sexy skintight jeans and a cashmere sweater. With both hands on her hips, Angie was much prettier than I remembered.

"Why are you wearing those stupid glasses?" asked her friend, Dana. I remembered Dana. She was a loudmouth and in everybody's business. I didn't like her much.

"And what happened to you calling me, dude?" Angie asked. "Did you lose my number?"

"I, uh…" I didn't have a chance to respond because they were tag-teaming me.

"Why are you here anyway?" asked Dana. "Don't you go to that artsy school now?"

"Yes, I did lose your number," I told Angie, completely ignoring Dana's question, "but I would love to have it again. Maybe I can call you sometime."

"Cool." She grabbed an ink pen out of her purse, took my hand in hers and began to scribble her phone number into the palm of my hand. "Plug it into your phone before you wash your hand, okay?"

"Okay," I said.

I admired her body as she stepped down from the bleachers, remembering that my attraction to Angie had been totally physical. She had the dumb-blonde thing going on.

"Why didn't she just let you plug the number into your phone right then, dude?" Preston asked the question that I was thinking.

"Don't ask stupid questions."

We both laughed.

Right before the game ended, I made my way to the floor and toward Coach Austin. After losing to Breckinridge, I knew that he'd probably be in a bad mood and the reunion might be a little painful. But it was something that I had to do. They'd lost but played a great game, losing by only one point. But if I knew Coach Austin, a loss was still a loss in his eyes. When I approached, he was shocked to see me.

"Bishop!" he yelled like a boot camp sergeant. It was the same voice that I often heard while running down the court and he wanted me to be somewhere else. It was always startling when he said my name. *Bishop!*

"Hey, Coach."

"You left without saying goodbye. What's wrong with that picture?" he asked. He often talked in what seemed like riddles. Or asked questions that he really didn't expect an answer to.

"I should've said goodbye?" It was more a question than a response.

"Darn right you should've said goodbye. That was a wimp move."

"Sorry?" Again a question.

"You left all of this—" he motioned toward the basketball court "—to go play house at that school in Manhattan."

"I, um… I went to pursue my dreams of acting."

"Whatever." He was insensitive. "You ready to come back and play ball or what?"

"Nah, Coach. Not right now."

"Okay, well, when you come to your senses, give me a call." He turned his back to me. "Okay, you little girls… let's get to the locker room. I got some stuff I wanna talk to you about."

"Congratulations on playing a great game," Preston said to Coach Austin.

Coach Austin turned around and gave Preston a strange

look. "A great game? What do you mean, great game? We lost!"

"You lost by one point," Preston explained.

"Whether it's ten points or one point, we still lost," he said and then marched toward the locker room. Left us both standing there without words.

"That went well," Preston said as we left the gym.

"I'll say."

"Well, if it isn't Benedict Arnold. I mean, Drew Bishop," said Antwoine, my friend and former teammate.

"What are you doing here, Drew?" asked Kev, one of my best friends since elementary school. It felt strange that he was greeting me this way—as if we hadn't slept over at each other's houses since we were small.

"Yeah, man, what are you doing here?" Andre asked. "This is no place for a sellout." His remark stung even more because I had known him since fifth grade, and considered him a close friend.

"Oh, so I'm a sellout because I decided to pursue my dreams?" I asked.

"This was supposed to be our year to shine, man. Basketball is what we do. Not Shakespeare," said Kev.

The three of them continued to take shots at me, and I didn't know how to defend it. I felt like Benedict Arnold. As if I'd betrayed everyone. Facing Coach Austin had definitely been something I wasn't prepared for. Before the game, I wasn't even sure I'd made the right decision— transferring to Premiere. But after my short-lived conversation with my former coach and my friends, I knew even more how important pursuing my dream was. If playing a good game didn't account for anything, as Coach Austin had said, then I was in the wrong place. And if my friends couldn't support my decision, no matter what it was, then they weren't my friends at all.

I felt more resolved with my decision as I hopped into the passenger seat of Preston's car.

nine

Marisol

The portable stereo was plugged into the wall. Jasmine and I danced to the sounds of Justin Bieber in an empty dance studio. When we mentioned that we were planning to audition for Dance America, J.C. had given us permission to use the studio during our lunch period in order to practice our routine. She thought it was wonderful that two of her students were auditioning for the competition. She even offered to help with our choreography if we needed her to. We took her up on the offer; we could use all the help we could get. With the Dance America auditions in one week, we had a lot of work to do.

J.C. showed us a few of her dance moves; moves that I couldn't believe she owned. She was graceful, and somewhat funky. She moved as the dancers did in some of the videos I'd seen on MTV, but with style. As we followed her lead, she taught us things that we would never have come up with on our own. With moves like this, we would definitely be taken seriously in the competition. We would look like professionals.

"From the top girls…one, two, three…" she said after slipping a different CD in. She had become our self-appointed choreographer. "The bass in this song is stronger and will work better for your routine."

In just a short time, she'd switched up our music as well as our routine. I kept thinking about Luz and how she wasn't able to join us. She would have a lot to learn in just a short time, but I had faith in her. She was not just an excellent dancer, but a quick study. If anyone could learn a dance routine in a short time, it would be her. I would show her every move, just as soon as I made it home from school. I'd already sent her a text and let her know that we were switching things up a bit, but that she would catch on quickly. She didn't respond, but I knew she would. She wasn't allowed to use her cell phone during class, but I knew she'd text me back in between classes. I couldn't wait to bring her up to speed.

As our lunch period ended, I wiped sweat from my brow with a small towel. I tossed the towel to Jasmine to wipe her sweat away. She started panting and coughing, and I couldn't help but think that it was because she smoked those horrible cigarettes. She'd be a much better dancer without them.

"You ladies really have potential," J.C. said, "but you don't have much time to work on this routine. So here's what I'm gonna do. I'll meet you here every day this week. Same time, same place. Which means you'll have to sacrifice your lunch hour."

"You mean you'll actually work with… Train us for Dance America?" I asked.

"Only if you want me to," she responded. "I would love to see someone from Premiere to actually take Dance America by storm. The potential is here."

Just listening to J.C.'s words had me excited inside. The thought of Jasmine, Luz and I making it to the finals gave me chills. I wished that Luz was a student at Premiere and could take advantage of the lunchtime rehearsals.

"There's a third member of this group. I wish that she could be involved, too," I explained. I didn't know if mentioning it would do any good. You never knew what strings grownups could pull.

"Does she attend Premiere?" J.C. asked.

"No. She attends a public school in Brooklyn—" I decided to reach for the moon "—but maybe we could do this in the evenings, and she could come by here after school."

"Won't work. I don't have much time to dedicate after school. This is the best time for me," she explained. "She's probably not going to work out as the third member of your group. Maybe you should consider just being a two-some."

"Well, we started out as a trio. And that's how we're gonna stay," I said. "I'll bring her up to speed."

"Whatever makes you happy," she said. "You should get dressed and get to your next class."

"We appreciate your help, J.C.," said Jasmine as she pulled a pair of jeans over her leotards.

"You're a lifesaver," I added.

"Glad to help," said J.C. as she removed her CD from the stereo and wiped sweat from her face with the sleeve of her shirt.

I put my jeans on and pulled my shirt over my head. Tomorrow I'd sneak my father's camcorder from its place on the shelf. I would videotape us as we danced our hearts out. With a dance coach like J.C., we truly had a chance at stardom.

I stepped into my advanced algebra class feeling great. My day was going well. I took my usual seat in the third row; fourth seat from the rear of the class. When Drew waltzed into my class and began searching for a seat, I wondered what was going on. He spotted me and took the seat at the desk right in front of me.

"What are you doing in this class?" I asked. We were well into the second week of school and I had never seen him in the class before.

"I got reassigned here," Drew explained. "They had me in some bogus math class at first. Funny seeing you here. Isn't this an advanced class?"

"Yes, it is." I'd always excelled at math.

"Shouldn't you be in a beginner's class?"

"I had those classes in middle school last year." I smiled confidently. He seemed uncomfortable. "Are you intimidated?"

"Of course not." He placed his palms over his ears. "There's more than just good looks in between these ears."

"You mean you have brains, too?" I asked.

"Sometimes I do."

I found myself staring at the face in between the ears. I was secretly thrilled to see Drew. It was refreshing. My heart pounded a few extra times as he grabbed my pencil pouch from my binder and began searching for a pencil. He wasn't ashamed to make himself at home with my things. Once a pencil was found, he grabbed my spiral notebook and ripped two sheets from it.

"I'll probably need this, too," he said.

"Help yourself," I said sarcastically.

With Drew in my algebra class, I wondered if I'd be able to concentrate. His presence seemed to distract me. As the instructor shut the classroom door and asked us to open our textbooks, I tried to forget that Drew was in the seat in front of me. I opened my algebra book and turned my spiral notebook to the first empty page. Drew passed me a note. I opened it—careful not to rattle the wrinkled piece of notebook paper.

MEET ME AT MANNY'S AFTER SCHOOL. GOT SOMETHING TO ASK YOU.

Got something to ask me? Why couldn't he just ask me whatever it was before the end of the school day? Why wait until we were at Manny's? I'd go crazy just trying to figure out what it was. What would Drew Bishop have to ask me at Manny's that he couldn't ask me in our algebra class?

The fall social was only a few weeks away. From what

I'd heard, it was a huge event for students at Premiere. Everybody dressed in tuxedoes and formal dresses, and sipped fruit punch from fancy glasses. Boys asked girls to be their dates for the evening, and they picked them up at their houses while parents snapped pictures of them with disposable cameras. If Drew was planning to ask me to the fall social, I'd need permission from my parents. I'd never been on a date before, and it would be very awkward for them. Poppy would definitely handle the news better. Mami wouldn't like it at all. She'd protest at first, but then Poppy would ease her fears; convince her that the world wouldn't end if I went on a date.

What would I wear? Luz and I would have to go to the mall immediately to pick out a dress. I'd have Grace pull out her nail kit and give me a manicure. Kristina would do my makeup. She'd been the best makeup artist since seventh grade. She'd practiced on us so many times. Luz would do my hair. Besides me, Luz was the master hairstylist. I'd have to decide if I wanted to wear lots of curls or if I'd put my hair up. It all depended on the dress I chose, I guessed.

My cell phone rested on my desk, and when it flashed, I knew that I had a new text message. I looked at the screen. Luz.

Let's go to the mall 2day. I want those boots.

Can't 2day.

Why?

Going 2 Manny's.

Manny's can wait.

Not 2day. How about tomorrow?

Whatever.

Luz seemed upset. I wanted to go to the mall with her, but there were more important things at hand—such as finding out what Drew had to ask me. After I had a chance to explain everything, Luz would understand why the mall would have to wait. I'd make it up to her.

As the bell sounded at the end of class, Drew packed his things.

"See ya later, kid," he said then made a beeline for the door.

He was so cute, I thought as I stuffed my things into my backpack. I took my time leaving the classroom; lost in thought. Anxiety had suddenly filled my world. I was anxious to get home and show Luz the new dance steps that Jasmine and I had learned. I was anxious to get back into the dance studio with J.C. and Jasmine to practice again. I was anxious to get to the Dance America auditions. And now, I was anxious to get to Manny's after school just to hear Drew's big question.

At Manny's I ordered a slice of pepperoni and a Cherry Coke. I slid into the booth next to Jasmine, who was already stuffing a slice of cheese pizza into her mouth. Drew and Preston walked into the door and headed our way. They dropped their things into the two empty chairs at our table.

"What's up, y'all?" Drew asked.

I shrugged; my mouth was filled with pizza.

"What's up, guys?" asked Jasmine.

Preston gave a wave, and then the two of them headed for the counter to order their pizza.

"I think Drew's going to ask me to the fall social," I told Jasmine. I immediately regretted saying it aloud. What if it wasn't true? What if he had something else to ask me instead? I'd be embarrassed.

"What are you going to say?"

"Um...probably yes." I smiled.

"You like him like that?" she asked. She seemed surprised.

I hadn't really shared my true feelings about Drew with anyone, except Luz and Grace. I'd only kept it inside; in my private thoughts—where no one could judge me. It wasn't that I really liked him all that much. I just liked the way I felt when he was around. It was as if we'd known each other forever; as though we'd met in another life.

"He's okay. I mean, he's a good friend," I said.

"Well, the fall social is a big deal at Premiere. Everybody goes, whether they have a date or not. I doubt that I'll have a date, but I'm still going," she explained. "If Drew doesn't ask, you can just go with me. No big deal."

No big deal? It was a very big deal, and becoming bigger by the moment.

Drew and Preston placed their pizza on the table. Preston turned his chair around and sat backward in it as he always did. Drew plopped down in front of me, stole the extra mozzarella cheese that was stuck to my plate and popped it into his mouth. He seemed to enjoy taking my things without asking; as if they belonged to both of us.

"Guess what?" he said to no one in particular.

"What?" Jasmine and I asked at the same time.

"Yours truly will be playing the role of Walter Lee Younger in the school's production of *A Raisin in the Sun*." He cleared his throat. "No applause, please."

"Congratulations," I was the first to say. I knew how important that role had been for him.

"That's fantastic, dude," Jasmine said. "You should be very proud. I know lots of people who auditioned for that role."

"She's right, dude," said Preston as he grinned at Jasmine. "You should be proud."

I was proud of Drew, and all the small talk was fine, but I wanted to get to the subject at hand—the big question.

"So is anybody going to the fall social?" I asked. I wanted to get it out there in the open before I burst with anticipation.

Drew looked around the table, as if he wondered the same thing. "What's the fall social?" he asked.

What's the fall social? Did he really ask that?

"It's one of the biggest social events at Premiere," Jasmine explained. "The fall social and the spring talent show are two events that you can't miss."

"I hadn't really thought about it. Preston and I might

show up or something, just to see what it's all about," Drew said and then turned to Preston. "You wanna go, man?"

"Sure. Whatever," said Preston.

"When is it?" Drew asked, his eyes moving back and forth between Jasmine and me, searching for an answer.

"It's in three weeks," said Jasmine. "The first Saturday in October."

"Shouldn't you have a date for these things?" Preston asked.

"It's just a dance," Drew said and finished off his slice of pizza. "It's not the senior prom or anything."

"People take dates, though, silly," Jasmine said.

"Do you have a date, Jasmine?" Preston asked. Apparently, he was tired of beating around the bush. He'd been dying to ask Jasmine out.

"Yes, I do!" she exclaimed. "My girl Mari and I are going stag. Right, Mari?"

"Right." I smiled on the outside but was disappointed inside to know that Drew had no intentions of asking me to go.

I appreciated Jasmine at that moment; rescuing me from embarrassment. I ate in silence. Couldn't believe I had allowed myself to be so silly, and over a guy who obviously wasn't interested in me. I wouldn't put myself in that position again.

"Oh, yeah, Mari. Got a question for you," said Drew.

Now he's got a question for me? What else is there besides "Mari, will you go with me to the fall social?"

"I'm listening," I said and picked over my pizza.

"It's kind of embarrassing," he started.

What could be more embarrassing then expecting a boy to ask you to a dance, and he doesn't?

"Spit it out, dude," Preston said.

"It's all good that I landed the role of Walter Lee Younger. But none of that makes any difference at all if I can't keep my grades up in math," he said. "I'm ashamed to say that at my old school, where I was a basketball idol, I didn't do much of my own homework. Girls came out of the woodwork...just waiting to date someone from the team. They did whatever you asked."

Was he asking me to do his homework for him?

"And needless to say, he took advantage of the poor souls," Preston teased.

"Anyways, I've turned over a new leaf. I'm not that basketball star anymore. And I want to do this on my own. I'm grateful for this opportunity at Premiere, and I sincerely want to remain a student here. But if I don't keep my grades up, I'll be out on the street."

"What does that have to do with me?" I asked.

"Will you help me pass math? You're obviously pretty smart if you're taking advanced classes," he said. "I won't require a lot of your time. Just a couple of hours a week. And I'll pay you."

"You mean like a tutor?" I asked.

"Yeah, something like that," he said.

"I don't have a lot of time," I explained. "I'm preparing

for Dance America right now. And we barely have enough time as it is."

Jasmine nodded her head in agreement.

"Just one day a week is all I need, Mari."

"Let me think about it," I told him. I wasn't going to be overzealous again. But I had to admit that the thought of spending one-on-one time with Drew was exciting. However, I wasn't sure how I'd pull it off. Having a slice of pizza at Manny's was one thing, but tutoring someone would require more time. What would I tell my parents?

"Let me know," he said. "No pressure. There are lots of people who would love the job, but it's gotta be somebody that I enjoy hanging out with. That's why I chose you."

I blushed at the compliment and hoped that nobody noticed. As I finished my Cherry Coke, I smiled to myself. I already knew that I'd tutor Drew, but I wanted to make him suffer. He deserved it for not asking me to the fall social. Didn't he know when he'd broken a girl's heart?

ten

Marisol

I was so excited, I nearly ran home from the subway station. I couldn't wait to get with Luz and go over our dance routine. My backpack in tow, I looked for any sight of Luz, Kristina and Grace as I turned the corner. The Block was empty, except for the younger boys popping wheelies on their dirt bikes.

"Where is everybody?" I asked Hector, Grace's younger brother.

"Fight broke out," he explained. "Some guys were trying to fight your brother."

"Nico?" I asked. "What guys?'

"Some gang members," Hector said. "Everybody's over there."

"Where?"

"The next block over."

I dropped my bag onto the steps of our two-family house and took off running to the next block. A crowd had gathered, and I spotted Kristina and Grace in the midst of it.

"What's going on?" I asked them.

"Some boys have beef with Nico," Kristina explained.

I pushed my way through to the center of it all. Alejandro and Fernando stood in the center with their arms folded across their chests. In the midst of the crowd, my brother argued with a guy dressed in sagging jeans, an oversize hoodie and a bandanna tied around his head. As I got a closer look, I realized it was Diego, the boy who I'd seen being arrested and thrown into a police car. Diego grew up in our neighborhood, yet somehow had taken a wrong turn. He was a gang member who had been in and out of the juvenile detention center since our first year in middle school. He and Nico were once good friends. Diego had spent several nights at our house, and our families had attended the same church. When Diego's father died of cancer, he was angry. Angry with his mother; angry at the world for allowing his father to die. He started rebelling and ended up in a gang. Rumor had it that he'd even killed a few people, although I couldn't imagine Diego hurting a fly. He was one of the quietest boys I'd ever known— straight-laced; very respectable. And why he was standing here in the middle of the street having an altercation with my brother was beyond me.

Standing in between Nico and Diego, I asked, "What's going on here?"

I was confused. Especially since I'd just seen Diego at the mall, and he had pledged his innocence. He'd talked about how the cops were always harassing him for nothing, yet he was standing in the middle of the street having an issue with my brother. I didn't know what to make of it.

"Go home, Mari. This has nothing to do with you," Nico yelled.

"It has everything to do with me. You're my brother!" I yelled and then turned to Diego. "Diego, what's going on here?"

"Do what your brother said, Mari, and go home," said Diego. "This is between me and him."

"You want me to take him out?" asked a guy who was standing behind Diego. He was someone I didn't recognize from our neighborhood. He was tall and wore a do-rag on his head. With tattoos plastered all over his neck and arms, and a permanent frown on his face, he said, "Nobody disrespects us like that."

I stood there, confused. How had Nico disrespected them? I wanted to ask, but it didn't seem as if they were up for much conversation. I quickly realized that talking was definitely not what Diego had in mind after I spotted the silver gun he held close to his side, with his finger strategically placed on the trigger. At that moment, my heart started pounding. I was the bravest girl in the world—standing in front of my brother, daring anyone to hurt him. But instantly, my knees began to shake and I wondered if Nico and I would both die in the middle of the street in front of all our friends. What would become of our parents if both their children were murdered in broad daylight? Mami wouldn't survive the tragedy, and Poppy would be heartbroken for the rest of his life.

Our parents had done their best to shelter us from the trouble that surrounded our Brooklyn neighborhood—gang activity, drugs and violence. In fact, there was a cluster of families in our neighborhood who had refused to allow the streets to destroy their children. The families on The Block were wholesome, working-class people with strict values. The parents had formed a pact to protect their children from the streets, and had done so for many years. Besides being neighbors for several years, we were one big family.

Diego's family had been a part of our big family—that is until his father was no longer around. Mr. Reyes had been the glue that held the family together, and once he was gone, Mrs. Reyes could no longer control Diego. She lost him to the streets. Eventually, Mrs. Reyes wasn't able to maintain their home and was forced to move to a one-bedroom apartment in Williamsburg. Diego had dropped out of school, so he was no longer classmates with any of the rest of us, and church wasn't an option for him anymore, either. His days of being an altar boy at our Catholic church were long over.

"This isn't over, Garcia," Diego said to my brother, as his finger slowly eased from the trigger. "You'll hear from me again."

Nico stood there, a mean mug on his face, as he stared at Diego, his eyes piercing. I wondered if he felt the same relief that I felt as Diego stuffed the gun into the pocket of his jeans and began to walk away.

"Let's go," Diego barked to his tall, tattooed sidekick. The two of them took off walking.

"Why did you do that?" Nico yelled at me.

"Do what?"

"Stand in front of me like that! You could've gotten us both killed." Nico was enraged.

"I didn't want you to get hurt."

"I don't need your help, Mari. I can fight my own battles." He started walking toward home—Alejandro and Fernando beside him.

I followed. "What was that all about anyway?" I asked.

"It doesn't have anything to do with you, Mari. Stay out of it!"

"I'm telling Mami and Poppy."

Nico stopped in his tracks. He grabbed my arm and gripped it tightly; gave me that same piercing look that he'd given Diego earlier. "You better not breathe a word of this to them. You understand me?"

I swallowed hard. Nodded my head yes. He eased the grip on my arm. I watched as he walked away and turned the corner toward home. Kristina and Grace caught up to me.

"Mari, that was so scary. I thought Diego was going to shoot Nico," said Grace, "and all because Nico refuses to join their stupid gang."

"Diego has changed a lot!" Grace added. "He's not the same boy that I kissed on my front stoop in first grade."

She'd kissed him, too?

"Is that what this is about? Nico won't join their gang?" I asked.

"I think he told them he would and then backed out," Grace explained. "I'm glad he reconsidered, because those guys are just bad news."

I sighed. I wasn't sure if I was more worried because gang members were hassling Nico for doing the right thing, or because he had considered joining them in the first place.

"Where's Luz?" I finally asked.

It was odd that she wasn't anywhere in the midst of the crowd. The entire neighborhood had gathered to see what was going on.

"She's at home," Kristina said. "She's locked in her room with Catalina Sanchez."

"Who's Catalina Sanchez?" I asked.

"You know, the girl who took the dance class with you and Luz last spring at the community center. She was like one of J.C.'s favorites in the class, always trying to outdo everybody," said Grace.

"She was the girl who wanted to beat you up last summer because she liked Fernando, and he wouldn't pay any attention to her because Fernando likes you," Kristina added.

"Fernando doesn't like me like that. He's like a brother to me," I explained.

"I hate to tell you, Mari, but Fernando doesn't want to

be your brother." Grace giggled. "He's liked you for a long time."

"What's Luz doing locked in her room with Catalina?"

"She and Luz have been pretty tight since you started going to Premiere. She doesn't even hang with us at school that much. It's always Catalina this, Catalina that," said Grace.

"I don't trust her," Kristina said. "Luz didn't tell you about Dance America?"

"Tell me what?"

"She and Catalina are dance partners now. They're trying out for Dance America together," Kristina explained.

"What do you mean? She's already trying out for Dance America with Jasmine and me. We already have a group. Brooklyn Bellezas. Remember?" I asked.

Grace shrugged. I could tell that she was trying to stay out of it.

"She claims that she's not a part of that group anymore," Kristina explained.

"When was she going to tell me?" I asked, and both Grace and Kristina shrugged.

"You know how Luz is sometimes, Mari. I wouldn't worry about it," said Grace.

Easier said than done. It bothered me that Luz would leave the group without even telling me. But worse than that, she'd already formed a partnership with someone else—someone she knew I didn't get along with. I walked just a little bit faster, headed for Luz's redbrick-front house.

I stomped up her stairs and rang the bell. She swung the door open. A bottle of Jarritos soft drink in her hand and her hair pulled up into a ponytail, she stood there with a smug look on her face. Just past her, I could see Catalina standing in the doorway of the kitchen, wearing leotards and patting her face with a towel.

"Hola," Luz said.

"What's this about you getting a new dance partner?" I asked. "What happened to the Brooklyn Bellezas?"

"That's your group, Mari. Yours and Jasmine's. I'm doing my own thing now," she said.

"When were you going to tell me?" I asked.

"I was going to tell you—" she looked over my shoulder and peered at Grace and Kristina "—it's just that the two big mouths beat me to it."

"I didn't say a word, Luz," Grace, the peacemaker, said.

"She deserved to know," Kristina said.

"So you're gonna go up against me in the competition?" I asked just to be clear about it.

My best friend since *forever* was now my opponent. It felt strange. It felt as if a part of me had begun to die right there on Luz's stoop—a stoop that I'd stood on so many days before, eating paletas and watching the older girls jump double Dutch, at least until we were old enough to jump, too. It was the same stoop where Luz and I shared our deepest, darkest secrets with each other—about boys, about how our bodies began to change during puberty and about life. We became blood sisters on that stoop; pricking our fingers with a safety pin and smashing the blood together. We were inseparable for life—at least that's what we promised.

"Hi, Mari." Catalina appeared in the doorway next to Luz.

The two of them grinned, and I walked away. I was fuming as I hopped down Luz's concrete steps and crossed the street toward my own house. Grace and Kristina followed.

"Don't worry about it, Mari. She's just jealous of your friendship with Jasmine." Kristina tried to console me.

"Yeah, just brush it off, Chica. She'll come around," Grace said.

I grabbed my bag from the stairs. "Thanks," I whispered to them before going inside.

I felt as if the world around me had come crashing down in a matter of minutes. How do you repair your world when it's shattered in a bunch of pieces?

eleven

Drew

With my backpack draped across my shoulder, I strode with Preston down West Forty-Second Street in the heart of Manhattan. Sometimes we just walked the streets of New York because we had nothing better to do. We ended up near McDonald's in Times Square, where loud music enticed tourists to come inside for a Double Quarter Pounder with Cheese. With the restaurant's bright lights, loud music and big-screen televisions, we couldn't resist going inside.

"Order me a chocolate shake," Preston said. "I gotta find the restroom."

He disappeared into the crowd of people, and I stood in the long never-ending line waiting to order Preston a shake and myself a large fries. Not that I needed to eat again after having pizza at Manny's, but who could resist McDonald's fries? Besides, the McDonald's in Times Square was always a nice place to meet beautiful girls who might be visiting the city for a weekend. You could always tell who the tourists were. They were the ones looking up at the skyscrapers, with their video cameras in hand. Or they were the ones who stopped in the middle of the sidewalk with no clue that they were holding up the foot traffic. You could always find tourists taking photographs with the life-size wax statue of Morgan Freeman or some other celebrity just outside the wax museum on West Forty-second Street.

Finally making it to the counter, I ordered Preston's chocolate shake and a large order of fries. I spotted Preston having a conversation with a blond-haired girl wearing a short miniskirt and a cropped top with her stomach hanging out. She definitely wasn't his type, and I could tell that she was invading his space.

Preston was reserved and laid-back. He was the guy who cared what girls were feeling or thinking, and he couldn't bear to see a girl cry. Which is why his last girlfriend, Dusty, had walked all over him. She mistook his kindness for weakness. From then on, any girl who he ended up with him had to meet my approval. I became his conscience. I was the one who reminded him that he had enough money and enough charm to have any girl in the state of New York, or New Jersey for that matter.

"You just can't be so eager, man," I'd told him. "You have to play hard to get a little bit. Make 'em work for the love."

"Make them work for it?" he'd asked with a laugh.

"You laugh, but I'm serious. That's why you're always heartbroken at the end of your relationships with women. You put too much of yourself into it. You can't give them your all—not all at once."

I think that he took my advice to heart, because right after that he dated three different girls all at once, and not one of them had captured his heart. From across the room it appeared that the blond-haired girl had accomplished what she'd set out to do: extort money from my very rich friend. He pulled out his wallet and pulled a bill out; handed it to her.

"Thanks," she said just as I walked up.

He gave her a grin, and I all but dragged him out of McDonald's by his hair. He'd lived in this area all his life, and he still seemed more like a tourist than a native. Being rich didn't allow you to interact with those who were less fortunate. Before Preston met me, he'd never even walked the streets of the city. He'd been chauffeur-driven most of his life—at least until he was able to drive himself around. Before last summer, he hadn't ever tasted a real New York hot dog from a street vendor or ate a slice of Italian pizza. He'd never ridden the subway, tasted Junior's cheesecake from the flagship Brooklyn restaurant or stopped for a latte at Starbucks in SoHo. He'd never been to any of the boroughs besides Manhattan. He'd been sheltered.

"What are you doing, man?" I asked after we were outside.

"She said she was hungry. Said she hadn't eaten anything in two days." He was serious.

"She was hustling you, man."

"Really? No."

"Yes," I said. "She didn't look hungry at all. If she hadn't eaten in two days, you should've taken her to the counter and bought her a cheeseburger instead of giving her cash."

"She said she was going to the counter and ordering her food right away."

I turned around just in time to see Preston's blond-haired friend walking quickly down West Forty-Second Street— no cheeseburger, no large fry, no chocolate shake.

"You see that?" I pointed her out. "She hustled you."

He laughed when he saw her. "She hustled me."

Wearing nothing more than our T-shirts, boxer shorts and tube socks, Preston and I shot hoops using a pair of dress socks as the ball and a makeshift basketball goal—a trash can. He tried with everything he had to block my shot, but I was too smooth. I maneuvered around him with precision and shot the socks into the trash can.

"Two points!" I yelled.

"You win," he said and then headed for the kitchen. "What you got to drink in here?"

I collapsed onto the sofa to catch my breath. ESPN was on mute on the flat-screen television, while Rihanna's sexy voice rang loudly through my dad's expensive speakers— a Caribbean-style song featuring Drake. I started dancing around the room as Preston tossed me a bottle of Gatorade. Having the house to myself for a weekend was not unusual, especially with a sportscaster father who traveled a lot. And it wasn't unusual for Preston to hang out at my place for the weekend, or for me to hang out at his.

Without any adult supervision, we'd probably find ourselves playing sock basketball until we were tired or bored; whichever came first. I'd teach him a few hip-hop dances and laugh when he actually tried to do them. Around midnight, we'd take a walk into Midtown and grab some Korean food or a couple of cannoli from the late-night Sicilian place on the corner. In the past, we'd walked over to ESPN Zone and played a few video games—that is, before they closed down in New York.

As we listened to Mister Cee on Hot 97's Friday Night Live, I bounced to the music. I had energy and the night was young. For some strange reason, I had an urge to talk to Mari; wondered what she was doing. With parents as strict as hers, she was probably in bed already. Unfortunately, I hadn't taken the time to get her cell phone number, so contacting her would be a long shot.

"So what you wanna do, man?" I asked Preston.

"I got a taste for pancakes," he said.

"Pancakes? At nine o'clock at night?" I asked.

"Yeah."

"There's IHOP or Junior's. Which one?" I asked.

"Junior's!" he exclaimed. "In Brooklyn."

"Why Brooklyn? There's a Junior's right here in Manhattan."

"I bet the pancakes are better in Brooklyn," he said and grinned, and then I knew. He was thinking of Jasmine and wanting to be close to her.

"Have you been talking to her?" I asked.

"Who?"

"Jasmine. That's who."

"Only at Manny's a couple of times. I would like to talk to her more, but I don't think she's feeling me."

"You gotta loosen up a little, man. You're too uptight. And you gotta be a little more assertive. Ask the girl for her number," I told him.

I'd watched him drool over Jasmine for days but never having the courage to ask her out. Whenever he threw any hints, she played him off. It seemed as if they were from two totally different worlds. Jasmine didn't seem refined at all. She smoked cigarettes, which was a huge turnoff. She was from Bed-Stuy, which was a place I was sure that Preston had never set foot in. And if he ever visited there, he'd stick out like a sore thumb. A preppy white dude wearing a pair of Calvin Klein jeans, low-top Converses and an expensive blazer, who didn't appear street-smart, shouldn't be casually walking around some streets in Brooklyn.

"I'll get around to it," he said.

"When?"

"As soon as you ask Mari for hers," he said matter-of-factly.

"What? I don't need her number," I said. "Well, maybe when she starts tutoring me in math…I'll probably need it then or something…"

"Do you realize that you always say *or something* when you're lying?"

"What? That's dumb."

"You do," he said with a smile. "You like her, and you know you like her. Why don't you just admit it?"

"I think she's cool. She's fun to hang out with...*or something*."

"Let's go to Brooklyn for pancakes," Preston said.

Before I knew it, Preston and I were dressed in old, grubby sweats and on the subway headed for Brooklyn. Using his computer expertise, Preston had located an address and phone number for Jasmine. He called her and she'd agreed to meet us at Junior's on Flatbush Avenue at midnight. For her to take the risk of sneaking out of the house that late, she was obviously as interested in Preston as he was in her.

Jasmine was already seated in a corner booth at Junior's, a small boy next to her—his jaws filled with pancakes as she wiped syrup from his mouth. She gave us a wave as we entered the restaurant.

"Hi," Preston smiled.

"Hi," she said. "I went ahead and grabbed us a booth."

"Thanks. That was very thoughtful," Preston said and slid in next to Jasmine.

I removed my Yankees cap and took a seat also.

"Who are you?" asked the little boy.

"Don't talk with your mouth full," Jasmine scolded him. "This is my little brother, Xavier. My parents work nights, so he had to tag along."

As I watched Jasmine and Preston nervously chitchat

about absolutely nothing, I found myself staring at her. She was pretty, but I honestly couldn't understand Preston's infatuation with her. There were several pretty girls who would jump at the chance to be with him. Girls who were much more refined and way prettier. But for this girl, he was willing to ride the subway to Brooklyn in the middle of the night and order nothing more than a Diet Coke.

They were so caught up in their conversation that Xavier and I were completely ignored. I was bored.

"So you got Mari's number?" I asked Jasmine.

"Why?"

"Because I wanna talk to her," I said. "Can I have it?"

"Hmm...I don't know. What do you need to talk to her about?"

"It's personal."

"I don't know if I should be giving her number out. Especially if you're planning on calling her right now."

"Well, maybe you can call her and ask her if it's okay."

She pulled her cell phone out of the pocket of her jacket; dialed a number.

"Hey, Mari, it's me, Jasmine..."

After talking about everything else, including the dances that they'd learned during their lunch hour that day, Jasmine finally got around to asking Mari if she could pass her number on to me. She gave me a look as she continued her conversation.

After hanging up, she looked my way. "She said it's cool."

I keyed Mari's number into my phone. I didn't want to

seem too anxious, so I waited around before calling; pretended that it wasn't that serious. In reality, I couldn't wait to get her on the phone. I wondered if there was any chance that I could see her before heading back to Manhattan.

"I'm gonna step outside for some fresh air." I made up an excuse to leave the table; needed privacy. I stepped out into the Brooklyn night air, pulled my cell phone out and dialed Mari's number. She picked up on the second ring.

"Hello," she said.

"What's up, kid?" There was a smile in my voice, and I tried to hide it. "It's Drew…from school."

"Hi." She sounded as if she'd been sleeping.

"Did I wake you?"

"Not really," she said, but I could tell that I had.

"Guess where I am."

"Brooklyn. Jasmine told me," she said. "What are you doing in Brooklyn?"

"It's Preston. He had a strong urge for Junior's pancakes…so…"

"So you came all the way to Brooklyn for pancakes?" she giggled. "There's a Junior's in Manhattan."

"Truth?" I asked.

"Truth."

"Okay, Preston wanted to see Jasmine…badly."

"Really? He must really like her."

"He does, even though he won't admit how much."

"So, you just tagged along for the ride?"

"Pretty much," I lied. "Any chance you can get out of the house?"

"Not a chance. They have chains on all the doors around here," she said and laughed. "But it's nice to know that you're so close."

Was she trying to pull my heartstrings? Because it was working.

"Okay, well, I guess I'll talk to you later. Even though it's Friday night and the night is still young...um..."

"Maybe you can call me when you get home," she said. "You know...just to let me know that you made it there."

"Okay, I'll do that."

"Okay."

"You're not going to be sleeping, are you?" I asked.

"I'll wait up," she said.

And with that, I went back inside. I was suddenly in a hurry to get home. I had a phone date—or something. Whatever it was, I was excited about it.

"Okay, bro. We need to get back to the city," I told Preston. "Let's wrap up this little rendezvous. Jasmine...nice seeing you again. Xavier, good to meet you..."

Xavier gave me a wide grin, and it was then that I noticed his missing two front teeth. I held my hand out, grabbed his little hand in mine and gave him a firm handshake.

"Stay in school," I told him.

"Okay." He giggled.

"So I guess I'll see you at Manny's on Monday," Jasmine told Preston.

"I guess so," Preston said, agreeing that Manny's would be their next meeting place. "Can I call you a cab or something?"

"No. We'll be fine." She smiled. "I'll see you later."

"Okay, Manny's on Monday."

"You can call me tomorrow if you want to," she told Preston.

"Can I call you tonight? Just to make sure that you and my new little friend here, Xavier, made it home safely." He gave Xavier a high five.

"You can call me tonight," said Jasmine.

I had to pry Preston kicking and screaming from Junior's. I slipped my Yankees cap back onto my head as we walked to the subway station.

twelve

Marisol

MY knees were locked and my hands trembled as I sat in the school's auditorium with the number 157 plastered across my chest. Several students were seated on the floor with their backs against the wall. Some of them stood in the back of the auditorium or in corners of the room with their arms folded across their chests. It was standing room only, and we were lucky to get a seat.

Jasmine sat calmly in the seat next to mine, sending text messages to someone. I suspected it was Preston. Over the course of a week, the two of them had become somewhat of an item. There was lots of flirting and giggling going on between them, but not much else. I wondered when he would have the courage to ask her out on a date. A real date—not just for a slice of pepperoni at Manny's. There was nothing special about that—everybody hung out there.

As her phone buzzed and she read the incoming message, I wondered how she could be so calm at a time like this. Tryouts for Dance America were huge and happened only once a year. Someone's life was about to change completely. The winner of a competition like this would no longer be the same. They would travel to Hollywood to star in a film being produced for release in the spring. And just this morning, I learned that Justin Bieber would make an appearance in the movie. This small fact caused my heart to dance. I would give anything to meet him in person.

As the noon hour quickly approached, we'd sat through fifty-nine routines so far. Being number 157 on the list meant that Jasmine and I probably wouldn't audition until well into the afternoon or early evening. It would be a long, tiresome process, but well worth it if we got past the first round. Round two would begin first thing tomorrow morning, and I'd already made plans to skip Sunday morning Mass at our church. It was a struggle to convince my parents to first allow me to compete, and second to allow me to skip church in the event that I made it past the first round. But ultimately they signed the permission forms and gave me the green light.

With my textbook in my lap, I'd planned on completing my science homework, but I was distracted by the events of the day. And with my upcoming American history exam, I needed to study, but who could study for a test when there was so much going on? I made a mental note to give American history and science my undivided attention once I made it home. I had to. If I didn't do well on the exam, it would affect my grade for the entire semester. I stuffed the textbook back into my backpack.

As the judges called number sixty-two on the list, I

watched as a familiar face suddenly appeared onstage. It was Luz. Or should I say Backstabber Luz? Her hair was pulled into a ponytail and she and Catalina wore matching outfits—a pair of sexy black shorts that didn't cover much skin and black T-shirts with CALIENTE written across their breasts in bold red letters. They danced to Willow Smith's song about whipping her hair—the same song that Luz had complained about when Jasmine had suggested it.

"I don't believe it," I whispered to Jasmine.

"Me either," she whispered back.

As Luz and Catalina snatched ponytail holders from their hair and began to toss their locks back and forth, the crowd went crazy. Although I was steaming mad at Luz at the moment, I couldn't help but admire their routine. They were good. There was no doubt that they'd make it through to the second round, which made me even madder. It had been a solid week since Luz and I had spoken. That was the longest we'd ever gone without talking. There were plenty of times when Luz and I would get mad at each other, but by the end of the day, all would be forgiven. Not this time. This time was different. With each passing day, the tension grew thicker and thicker, which made it that much harder to break the silence.

For a brief moment, I'd thought about asking Luz if she wanted to ride the subway into the city together. But when I glanced out my bedroom window at the crack of dawn that morning, I saw Catalina and her mother pull up in front of Luz's house. She ran out with a Pop-Tart in her hand and hopped into the backseat of the car. I had watched as they pulled away from the curb and then disappeared down the street. I was jealous. Catalina Sanchez had stolen my best friend.

They ended their routine with a sizzle as each of them touched their butts with their index fingers. As they jogged off the stage, the whistles and cheers seemed endless. Part of me had wished that they hadn't done so well. To my surprise, the duet had performed the best routine of the day. I knew that Luz was a good dancer, but I had no idea that Catalina had so much talent. I hated to admit it, but she was a better dancer than Luz.

"You're both through to the next round," I heard one of the judges say.

Luz and Catalina screamed and hugged each other before exiting the stage. As much as I hated to admit it, they both were really good, and they both deserved to move to the next round.

When my phone lit up, I looked down at the screen, secretly hoping it was Luz. I wanted to congratulate her, but I wanted her to be the one to break the silence. After all, it was she who owed me an apology. And I wouldn't accept it right away. No, I wanted her to work for it. Surprisingly, it was a text message from Drew.

How are tryouts going?

Lento (that means slow).

Ten paciencia.

OMG! Tú hablas español!

A little. Working on it.

I think that's sexy.

LOL! Then I should work harder at it.

Too bad ur not here.

Why?

4 moral support.

Find out the name of the person 2 ur right…

What??

Jus do it.

I wasn't sure what Drew was up to, but I did as he asked and introduced myself to the person who was seated to my right. She was a small girl, with long blond hair and silver braces on her teeth.

"It's a lot of people here today. Are you competing?" I asked her.

"Yes." She smiled.

"I'm Marisol…Marisol Garcia." I pretended to really be interested in making her acquaintance. "What's your name?"

"Sarah Jenkins," she said softly.

"Nice to meet you, Sarah. Good luck."

"You, too."

"What are you doing?" Jasmine whispered.

"Just introducing myself to the competition," I lied.

Jasmine leaned forward; looked past me and gave Sarah a glance. With a smirk on her face, she said, "Okay, whatever."

I opened my phone and sent Drew a text.

Her name iz Sarah Jenkins. Why?

He didn't respond right away, so I shut my phone and continued to watch the girl onstage who was doing a tap dance routine to an old Frank Sinatra song. I felt sorry for her. She was obviously confused about the type of competition this was. When the judges interrupted her routine in the middle, she was on the verge of tears.

"Are you Sarah Jenkins?" I heard someone ask. A red-headed boy with freckles stood at the end of my row.

"Yes," said Sarah.

"Someone needs you in the back. I think it's your mom," the freckle-faced boy stated.

"My mom's here?" Sarah asked and stood. She gathered her things and headed for the back of the auditorium.

Just as quickly as she left, Drew slipped into her seat; gave me a wide grin. *"Hola,"* he said.

"You dirty dog." I smiled. "You stole Sarah's seat."

"Stole is such an ugly word," he whispered. "Let's just say I borrowed it."

"What's up, Drew?" Jasmine asked. "What are you doing here?"

"I came for moral support," Drew said and then winked at me.

"These seats are reserved for participants in the competition," I told him. I wanted to save him the trouble of being thrown out of the auditorium once the ushers found out he wasn't a dancer.

Drew unzipped his hoodie. The number 217 was plastered across his chest. "I am a participant."

"You are too much, Drew Bishop," I told him.

"I know. I've been told that a lot."

Whatever anxiety I felt before Drew got there suddenly seemed to disappear. In an instant, he'd managed to ease my fears.

It was a mistake to look into the audience before the music started. I should've kept my head down instead and never faced the crowd, but someone whistled when Jasmine and I stepped onto the stage and I wanted to see who it was. As my eyes scanned the crowd, my heart started pounding ferociously and my legs trembled. I prayed that I could at least gain control of my legs—they were all I had at the moment, and I needed them to cooperate.

Wearing silver metallic halter tops and black baggy hip-hop pants, we stood onstage facing the audience. Our legs spread apart and our hands at our sides, we waited for the music to start. As our song rang out through the auditorium, my legs shook just a little less and the pounding in my chest eased just a little bit. Jasmine and I started moving to the music just as we'd rehearsed. We'd decided to incorporate a few pop-locking moves into our routine, just to spice it up a bit. I'd never pop-locked before, but I was able to pick up the moves after several hours of practice. Jasmine's father, who'd grown up in the eighties, had taught her the moves and then she taught me. The pop-locking part of the routine turned out to be the best part and a big hit with our newfound fans, which were applauding and whistling in the audience. I couldn't tell if we'd impressed the judges or not, because their faces were like stone; no expressions whatsoever. However, we ended our routine with a bow and exited the stage. We both sighed, relieved that we'd made it through the routine without either of us fainting.

The judges began filling out their scorecards and holding them in the air. The first judge gave us a full score of ten, and the second judge gave us an eight. The pounding in my heart started again as we awaited the third score. We needed at least another eight and we were through to the next round. It was as if the white male judge with salt-and-pepper hair wanted to see us sweat, so he took his sweet time in revealing his score. I crossed my fingers behind my back and held my breath.

"You girls work very well together, but the next round is a solo routine," he said. "I loved how you incorporated the pop-locking into your routine. It was very original. You're both very good dancers, but so are plenty of other people here today. You have to have an edge, something that sets you apart from the rest. So because of your originality, I gave you an eight. You're both through to the next round."

I stopped holding my breath and sighed with relief. Jasmine and I grinned and gave each other a high five, holding hands in the air for a few seconds; savoring the moment.

J.C. met us backstage. "That was awesome!" she exclaimed.

"Thank you for all your help," I told her.

"We couldn't have done it without you," Jasmine said.

"We're not done yet. We still have work to do. This is just the first round. You still got two rounds to go," J.C. reminded us. "We start work again on Monday, right?"

"Yes!" I said, grateful that she was still willing to work with us.

"Then I'll see you on Monday." She smiled and gave us both a hug.

As we made our way through to the back of the auditorium, people were congratulating us and offering high fives. People who we didn't even know were telling us how great we were and cheering for us. It was a great day.

"You were good, Mari," said a familiar voice. "Congratulations."

It was Luz. She was leaning against the wall with her new sidekick, Catalina.

"Thanks. So were you," I told her.

"The next round will really reveal who has talent," Catalina smirked.

Before I had an opportunity to respond to Catalina's comment, someone grabbed me from behind and lifted me into the air.

"Woo-hoo!" Drew spun me around in a circle before letting me down. He grabbed my hand and Jasmine's and pulled us both toward the door. "Let's go celebrate!"

Whatever negativity had awaited me back there in the auditorium that day, Drew had rescued me from it, and I was grateful. I was on such a high that I was glad that Catalina hadn't gotten the chance to bring me down. I wanted to stay in this place for a moment. Even if I didn't make it through to the next round, I still had this day...this moment...this time.

thirteen

Drew

strolling through Times Square was much more interesting this time. With Mari next to me, her long black hair pulled into a ponytail, we stopped at Starbucks and stood in line.

"What are you having?" I asked.

"I don't really drink coffee...not usually. I don't even know how to order a drink at Starbucks. It seems complicated," she said.

"It's not really. But you can tell the difference between the professionals and the rookies," I told her.

"How?"

"Don't ever walk into Starbucks and ask for a small, medium or large anything," I explained, "then everyone will know you're just a rookie. And you should already know what you want before you step up to the counter. You don't spend minutes scanning the menu. The people in line behind you are in a hurry to get wherever they're going, and they don't have time to wait on you to figure out what you want."

She giggled, and it was then that I realized that she had a tiny dimple in the left corner of her chin.

"What are you having?"

"Today I'm having a Venti Double Chocolaty Chip Frappuccino, with caramel drizzled on top of the whipped cream, and a shot of vanilla," I said. "Venti is the biggest size they have."

"That sounds good. I'll have the same thing. Only I'll take the smallest size they have."

"Cool," I said and stepped up to the counter.

Ashley was the cashier. She was tall and beautiful, and even more so in her Starbucks uniform. She wore her hair down today, and had makeup on her face. It had been days since I'd stopped in for a Frappuccino, and I was sure she'd missed seeing my face. It was no secret that Ashley wanted more than a coffee relationship with me; she wanted to be my girlfriend. But I wasn't ready to settle down at the moment; I needed to focus on school. And I wasn't sure that Ashley was the right girl for me, anyway.

She almost gave me a smile, until she saw Mari. She gave her a quick scan, frowned and then turned to me. "What can I get for you?

"The same thing I always get," I told her.

"Which is what?" She had an attitude, and it didn't look good on her. She was way too beautiful to be frowning.

She knew what I wanted. I ordered the same thing every time I came in.

"Two Double Chocolaty Chip Frappuccinos, with caramel drizzled on top of the whipped cream, and a shot of vanilla…one tall and one venti."

"Just a small for me," Mari whispered. "Tall is too big."

"Tall is small," I said and laughed. "Remember the crash course I just gave you?"

Mari laughed, too. Ashley frowned.

"Will that be all?" she asked with attitude.

"Will that be all?" I asked Mari.

"Yes," she said.

Ashley took two cups, scribbled my name on one.

"What's her name?" she asked.

"Mari," I said.

"What?"

"Mari," I said slowly.

"Spell it."

"M-A-R-I," I told her.

She scribbled Mari's name on the second cup. She gave me a price and I paid for Mari's and mine. Before she could hand my change over good, she was already looking over my shoulder at the next customer. "Next!" she exclaimed.

We'd been dismissed. And I knew I'd receive a nasty text message soon.

In two oversize, cozy chairs in a corner of the store, Mari and I sat facing each other and sipping on iced coffees.

"Is that your girlfriend or something?" she asked.

"Who, Ashley? Nah, she's just a girl that I know. She would like to be my girlfriend."

"But what?"

"But I'm not really looking for a girlfriend right now. Gotta focus on school and other things."

"She's the girl from Manny's that day. Are you leading her on?" Mari asked.

"What?" *Where did that question come from?*

"You know, are you making her think that she's your girlfriend…but because she comes with benefits, you just kinda let her believe it."

"No. I've been up front with her. She's just really into me," I said. "What should I do to let her know that I think she's cool and all, but I'm not really interested?"

"Just tell her."

"I did that."

"As long as you're not making it confusing for her, then there's nothing more you can do," she said.

"What about you? You got some guy chasing after you?" I asked. I wanted to know what Mari's status was—she was beautiful, talented and smart. I was sure that guys were beating her door down.

"Just my brother's friend, Fernando, who's had a crush on me since grade school," she said. "No real guys."

"Fernando's not a real guy?"

She giggled. "Fernando's a real guy, but he's more like a brother. We grew up together."

"Oh, okay. So when you say a *real guy,* you mean someone like me, right?"

"Yeah, something like that."

I pretended to wipe sweat from my brow. "Whew! Glad I'm a real guy."

"Okay, smarty-pants. How about you pull out your algebra book and we get started. I gotta get home soon," she said.

Mari had agreed to tutor me after school three days a week. I figured Starbucks would be a quieter place to study, and we'd avoid the hustle and bustle at Manny's. We pulled our books out, opened them up and began our first lesson together. It was hard to focus, because I was too busy admiring Mari's vanilla-colored skin. I wasn't ready to admit that she was hard to ignore. That I thought about her when she wasn't around. I wanted to learn algebra and be able to do my own homework and make my own grades. But more than that, I wanted to spend time with Mari.

After our session was over, Mari and I dumped our empty cups and walked out into the fall New York air. We headed down Broadway, and I walked Mari to the subway station. I wanted to bring up the subject of the fall social again. Wanted to ask her to go, but I wasn't sure if she would be willing to go with me. Or if her parents would even allow her to attend a dance with a boy. So I dropped it. If I was going stag and she was going stag, there was a good chance that we'd run into each other there anyway. So I let it go.

"You don't need me to ride into Brooklyn with you, do you?"

"No, I think I can manage from here," she said and smiled. "I'll see you at school tomorrow."

"Okay, kid. Don't forget to send me a text message and let me know that you made it home."

"I will."

I stuffed my hands into the pockets of my hoodie and watched as she took the stairs down into the subway station; her backpack draped across her shoulder, she never looked back. After she was no longer within view, I took off down Broadway toward home.

Dad was in sweats and a T-shirt; his legs stretched across the ottoman while the sportscaster on ESPN talked about last night's game.

I stuck my head into the family room. "What's up, Dad?"

"Hello, son. How was school?"

"It was really good. How was work?"

"Not bad," he said. "I got tickets to Friday night's game. Maybe you and Preston can go. I'll arrange for a car to pick you guys up."

"How about me and you?" I asked. I missed the days that Dad and I hung out. When I was younger, we went to all the Yankees' home games, all the Knicks games and all the Broadway shows together. I missed those days. His job seemed to absorb most of his time, and our time together had become less and less of a priority in his life.

"Gotta work," he said. "Sorry, son. I'll make it up to you. I promise."

"It's cool, Dad." I let him off the hook. "I landed the role in an off-off-Broadway play...I'll be playing Walter Lee Younger in *A Raisin in the Sun*."

"I've been meaning to talk to you about that, son."

"About *A Raisin in the Sun?*"

"About that performing arts school." He raised up in his seat. "When I gave you my approval, I didn't think you were really serious."

"I was pretty serious, Dad."

"And you're honestly not interested in playing ball anymore?"

"I still like basketball, Dad. That hasn't changed. I'm sure I'll play again. Maybe in college," I assured him. "Right now I want to focus on acting."

My dad shook his head; didn't really respond to my last comment.

"We'll probably be performing the play around Thanksgiving. You think you can come check it out?" I asked.

"I don't know, Drew. Maybe if I'm not working."

I was willing to accept that. At least he didn't say no.

"Okay, cool. I'm gonna go hop in the shower. Are we ordering takeout for dinner?"

"I brought Chinese home. All your favorites. Orange chicken and moo shu pork."

"Egg rolls, too?"

"Of course. Can't have Chinese food without egg rolls, right?"

"Right."

I was disappointed. I wanted my father to be excited about Premiere. I wanted him to understand how talented his son was, and not just with a basketball in hand. I had other talents, and if he'd just give me a chance, he'd see. I hoped that he would come around someday.

I hopped into the shower; let the warm water cascade over my face. When I heard my phone chirp, I hopped out of the shower, stumbled over my Jordan tennis shoes and stubbed my toe on the edge of the bed. I'd been patiently awaiting a text message from Mari. She promised to let me know when she made it home. I grabbed the phone from my nightstand. It was a text message from Ashley.

PUNK.

That was all she said. The four-letter word cut deep. It caused me to look inward—wonder if I was really behaving like a punk. I had been up-front with her. I told her from the beginning that she was beautiful and I liked being around her, but that I wasn't looking for a serious relationship. I probably shouldn't have spent the night at her house when her parents went away for the weekend. I guess that might've caused some confusion. I didn't think it meant that we were in a committed relationship.

I didn't respond. Instead I sent a text to Mari.

Make it home?

Sí.

Cool.

Busy?

No. What's up?

I *was* busy. I was still dripping wet from hopping out of the shower, but I had time for Mari. When my phone rang, I answered it on the first ring.

"I'm nervous about the second round of tryouts on Sat-urday," she announced.

"Why are you nervous? You're a great dancer."

"So is everybody else who made it through to the next round. The competition will be that much tougher this time."

"It just means you gotta work harder, kid. Can't slack this time."

"I didn't slack the first time." There was laughter in her voice.

"I bet you didn't give 110 percent," I said. "You probably only gave ninety-five. This time, Mari, you gotta bring it."

"I know," she said. "I just needed to hear it. Thanks for listening to me, Drew. I usually talk about these things with my best friend. But my best friend is not really my best friend anymore. She's my competitor."

"What do you mean?"

"Remember the girls in the competition with CALIENTE plastered across their chests…the ones who made the crowd go crazy?"

"Oh, yeah, the hot girls with the sexy little shorts on," I said, and Mari was silent for a moment. "Oops, did I say that out loud?"

"Yes, you did," she said.

"Sorry."

"That was my ex–best friend and some girl that I can't stand."

"Why isn't she your best friend anymore? What happened?"

"The competition happened," Mari explained. "And now, we'll be competing with each other in the second round."

"And what exactly is the problem?" I asked.

"It's just uncomfortable, that's all."

"Then you'll just have to win, that's all. She doesn't have anything you don't have. They were good, but you and Jasmine were better. And with a lot of work, you can beat them…easily."

"You think so?"

"I know so."

"Thanks, Drew. Thanks for trying to cheer me up," she said.

"Did it work?"

"Not really, but I appreciate you trying."

"Your best friend will come around. Just give it time. If she's your real friend, then you'll work it out. Otherwise, she's probably not your friend anyway and no love lost. Right?"

"I guess so," she said. "I have to go. My mom's calling me for dinner. I'll call you later."

"Okay. That's cool."

I sat on the edge of my bed for a moment—still wet from

jumping out of the shower. My heart went out to Mari. I wished I knew how to help her, but I didn't have any answers. There were times when Preston and I got into it, but before the end of the day we were friends again and I couldn't tell you what we were fighting about. Girls were different. They held on to things a lot longer. They took things to a different level, and made things worse than they really were. But I knew that Mari and her friend would work it out. Who could stay mad at her?

I hopped back into the shower; finished what I'd started. Closed my eyes and rehearsed my lines for the play.

fourteen

Marisol

saturday. The big day. The day of all days. It was the second round of Dance America. During this round forty people would be eliminated and ten people would remain and go on to the finals. Ultimately, the last person still standing at the end of the competition would go on to become famous—or at least, that's what was expected. After starring in a role on the big screen, how could you not become famous?

My fingernails were gnawed down to nothing, and my knees shook a little. I chewed on a couple of TUMS, hoping to settle the rumblings going on in the pit of my stomach. I reclined in my seat and took a look at Jasmine, who was seated next to me. As she sent text messages from her cell phone, she wasn't nearly as nervous as I was. She was cool and calm, like a rock.

"How can you be so calm?" I asked Jasmine. "Aren't you a little bit nervous?"

"A little. But it's not that serious."

"It is for me," I told her. "This is everything I could've

ever dreamed of, Jas. Do you realize that this could change our lives…forever?"

She looked up from her phone and smiled. "Victory is sweet. And yes, I've dreamed of winning. With the scholarship money, I could pay my own way to college and take some pressure off of my folks. But we can't let our nerves get the best of us. We have to remain calm and just do our best. We have to remember everything that J.C. taught us, and go out there and nail it."

"What college will you use the money for?" I asked. Mostly I wanted to take my mind off the competition and focus on something else.

"Julliard, of course." She grinned. "What about you, Mari? Where are you going to college?"

"Umm. I hadn't really thought about it much. I'm just a freshman. I have time to figure it all out."

"I thought that everyone who attended Premiere was Julliard-bound."

"I know it's a good school."

"It's only the most prestigious performing arts college in the world. And it's right here in the city. It's just a train ride from Brooklyn."

"Don't you want to go away somewhere? Get away from everything that you know and discover the world?"

"Not really."

"I do," I told her. "I want to discover what life is like outside Brooklyn. I wanna go somewhere like California or somewhere abroad."

"I want to stay right here in New York…my home…the place where I was born and bred. No place like it."

"That's true. But my parents drive me crazy with their strict rules. They don't give me any room to breathe. I can't wait until I'm an adult and able to make my own decisions." I propped my feet up on the back of the seat in front of me. "I live for that day."

I watched as Luz took the stage, wearing black shorts and a red cropped top. With her hair pulled into a ponytail, she shook to the music. I waited for that original move; the one thing that would send the crowd into a frenzy—the one thing that would set her apart from the rest, but there was nothing. Nothing was original about her routine. She was just shaking her booty as everyone before her had done. After she took a bow, I was shocked to know that her routine was over. Especially since she'd done so well during the first round.

"Not bad for an amateur." Celine pushed her way toward my legs, pushing them down from the seat in front of me. "You have to bring your A game to a competition like this."

"Diva. What's up?" asked Jasmine.

I didn't have the energy to endure Celine before going onstage. She'd made the top fifty, and had already performed her earth-shattering performance.

"Everything is wonderful. Just waiting for this competition to be over so that I can pack my bags for Hollywood," she said.

"How do you know that you're going to Hollywood?" Jasmine asked.

"Did you see my routine?" she asked—not really expecting an answer. "Your routine was okay. I liked the pop-lock thing you had going on last week. But I hope you got another bag of tricks up your sleeves today."

As she tossed her hair to one side, I hoped she wasn't going to stick around. She was like a snake releasing her venom on us, and we didn't need that at the moment. She was attacking my confidence, which was probably her goal. I stood. I wanted to get as far away from Celine as possible, so I headed for the ladies' room. I didn't have to go, but I took a look at myself in the mirror; freshened my lip gloss. I took a deep breath and glanced at the door as it swung open.

Luz walked in. "Hey," she said.

"Hey," I responded and waited for her next comment.

She said nothing more. Just stepped into one of the stalls. I stood there and waited for her to finish. We had a lot to talk about, and I was okay with discussing it right there in the girls' bathroom. When she came out of the stall, she stepped to one of the sinks, turned on the water and washed her hands. Just as I was about to start a conversation, Catalina walked in.

"That last act really sucked," Catalina said. "You should've seen their finale. It was terrible."

"Oh, yeah?" Luz seemed uninterested.

"Yes, girlfriend." Catalina walked over to Luz. "You

should wear your hair up…like this." She pulled Luz's hair up on her head.

"I don't want to wear my hair like that. I'm cool with it being down."

Luz was growing tired of Catalina already. I could tell. I knew Luz better than anyone, and I knew that she was at the point of barely tolerating her. She needed her to win the next round of competition, which was why she was still around. Catalina could never take my place. I knew it. Luz knew it. And soon Catalina would know it. She was on her way to being kicked to the curb, and she didn't even realize it yet. I chuckled inside at the thought.

I pushed my bangs out of my face, took one last glance into the mirror and walked out of the restroom. Just as I stepped into the auditorium, my number was being called. I found my way to the stage. I said a little prayer before taking my place on the buffed shiny floor. My head down as I awaited the music, all fear went out the window. Confidence took over as the music resonated through the room. As I performed steps that J.C. had so graciously given me, I knew that I'd make it to the final ten. Into my hip-hop routine, I incorporated a salsa move, a bit of merengue and a snippet of bachata—all Latin dances. The crowd was hysterical.

J.C. met me backstage, just as she'd done before. She hugged me.

"That was phenomenal!" she exclaimed.

"You think so?" I asked.

"Are you kidding?" she asked. "Yours and Jasmine's acts were the best all day!"

She was right. The judges said the exact same thing—ours were the most original and the best of all fifty acts. It felt good hearing them say that, but it felt even better at the end of the competition when they announced the winners. Jasmine and I were both through to the next round. I was beside myself with excitement when they called us to the stage to stand next to the other eight people who'd made it. It was as if I was having an out-of-body experience.

I watched as Luz and Catalina watched from the seats below. Unfortunately, they hadn't been chosen to move forward. My heart went out to Luz. I knew that she'd given her all, and I hated to see my friend lose. Even though we weren't speaking, I still cared about her. I didn't want to see her hurt.

As Celine ran her fingers through her hair, I wanted to stick my tongue out and give her the middle finger. She had already expressed her anger toward the judges and demanded a rematch, but to no avail. The judges had made their selections, and she wasn't included. She was angry. When she looked my way, I smiled. And as we exited the auditorium, I brushed against her.

"Next time you should bring your A game," I told her and grinned.

She snarled and rolled her eyes; walked on.

Life was good.

★ ★ ★

My parents weren't quite ready for the news of my advancing in the competition. They never expected me to make it as far as I had, so finding the right words was tough for them.

"I'm glad for you, Mari," Poppy said sincerely.

"And what exactly does this mean?" Mami asked.

"It means that Jasmine and I are in the top ten. If we make it to the top five, we get to go to Hollywood and compete for a dance role in a real live movie."

"Seriously, Mari?" asked my brother, Nico. "Are they going to cover your face up so you don't break the camera if you win?"

"Shut up, stupid." I frowned.

"Nico, leave your sister alone," Poppy said.

"So how long will this Hollywood thing last? How long will you be gone? And how will you travel there? And will you need our permission? And what type of movie is this anyway?" Mami asked too many questions. I wondered if she had plans of raining on my parade.

"I haven't won yet, Mami. Can we talk about it after I win?" I asked.

She didn't really answer. Instead she had a worried look on her face as she walked away; headed for the kitchen. Allowing me to attend Premiere was one thing, but now this. Dance America wasn't quite in the plans before now, and she was worried.

"Mari, I don't know about you going clear across the

country like that. California is a long way from here," she finally said. "What about school?"

"It's only a few days, Mami. And the school arranges for you to complete your assignments…so I won't really miss anything. Also, the competition pays for everything."

"What happened with Luz?" Nico asked. "I heard that she and Catalina made it through last week."

"She was eliminated today," I told him.

"Luz was eliminated?" Mom asked. "I thought the two of you were dancing together."

"We were…"

"Luz dumped Mari for Catalina."

"She didn't dump me…"

"And now the two of them aren't speaking."

"You're not speaking to Luz? Why?" Mami asked. "She's been your best friend since elementary school…as long as we've lived in this neighborhood. Is this competition changing who you are, Mari?"

"Mami! Luz stopped speaking to me…for no reason at all. Not the other way around. It's her who's changing!"

"Mari," Mami said.

"May I be excused?" I asked. I was getting frustrated and I needed a retreat. My parents didn't understand anything. I needed to be free—to spread my wings. And it seemed that they were preventing me from flying. Why couldn't I have parents like Jasmine's? Parents who didn't care what I did.

"Yes, you may be excused, sweetheart," Poppy said.

I left the kitchen and headed for my room. Collapsing on the bed, I covered my head with my pillow. Hoped for sleep. When someone tapped on the door, I knew that I wouldn't find peace anywhere.

"Mari," my father whispered as he stuck his head inside my bedroom door. "May I come in?"

I nodded.

"Mari, your mother is just worried about you. I know she can be difficult at times."

"Difficult is not the word, Poppy. You know her."

"I'm proud of you. This is quite an accomplishment," he said and smiled.

"You mean it?"

"Of course I mean it. You should be very proud of yourself. I've heard a lot about this uh…this Dance United States…"

"Dance America."

"Yes. I know that it's a tough competition, and that this is a wonderful opportunity for you, *mi amor,*" he said, "and we will support you."

"Thanks for your support, Poppy. But I know that Mami doesn't feel the same way."

"She'll come around. Just give her time," Poppy explained. "And this thing with you and Luz…it will work itself out."

"You think so?"

"I know so."

Poppy grabbed my nose in between his two fingers then

kissed my forehead. He always knew how to make me feel better. Even if I didn't win the competition, it was nice knowing that I had his support.

fifteen

Drew

I straddled my seat backward at Manny's; joined the rest of the gang that was already engaged in a conversation about the dance competition. Dance America had become the biggest conversation piece ever. That's all everyone talked about these days. Everyone had their opinions about who had won, who should've won and who had made it by the skin of their teeth. They talked about which contestants should've been eliminated, and which ones should've been given a second chance.

"I don't know if I should sit here...you know, amongst royalty and all," I teased Mari and Jasmine. "Pretty soon they won't even know us, Preston."

"I know. Once they get to Hollywood, we'll be a distant memory," Preston agreed.

"We'll have to make an appointment just to hang out with them," I added. "And forget about pizza at Manny's anymore. This place will be below their standards."

"The two of you need to stop!" Jasmine said with a laugh. "It's not even like that."

"I'd better take a picture with my camera phone—*a before-fame* photo." I snapped a photo of Mari and Jasmine with my phone.

"Yeah, let me get one, too." Preston pulled his iPhone out of the pocket of his jeans; snapped a picture of them also. Showed it to me.

"Hmm. That's a good one." I grabbed Preston's iPhone; showed Mari and Jasmine their photo.

"We owe our dance instructor all the credit. She taught us everything we know," Mari said.

"Well, I didn't see J.C. out there shaking her booty. It was you guys out there doing all the work," I said, "and I'm proud of you. You both deserve to win this competition."

"Okay, what's the punch line?" Mari asked before stuffing the last bite of her pizza into her mouth.

"No punch line. I'm serious," I explained.

I was serious. They had been the best dancers in the entire competition. I didn't realize that Mari could move like that. The more I watched her dance, the more attractive she became to me—and she didn't even know it. I wondered if she knew that I thought she was beautiful and cool. I watched as she laughed about something funny that Preston said. As she brushed a piece of hair from her face, I stared. And then caught myself; looked away. Didn't want her to catch me looking.

I stepped into our apartment; locked the door behind me. Dropped my backpack at the door and took a step across the hardwood floor.

"Pick it up!" a voice rang out in the apartment. "And take those sneakers off!"

The smell of laundry detergent mixed with the smell of fried chicken filled the place. And just as I started to untie the shoestrings on my sneakers, Gram popped her head into the entryway. With her salt-and-pepper hair and beautiful skin, she smiled.

"Hi, Gram." I grinned from ear to ear. "I didn't know you were coming."

It was always nice when Gram showed up. She always seemed to get us organized and to whip us into shape. And she always made the best meals—fried chicken or smothered pork chops. She usually left us with three or four casseroles that would last for a week or so, fresh white socks and clean underwear. Our linens would smell like Bounce dryer sheets, and she would even clean in between the cracks and crevices of the bathroom tiles and bathtub—getting rid of all the soap scum.

"Come here and give me a hug, boy," she said. I hugged my grandmother, and she returned the hug with a tight squeeze and a kiss on my forehead. She grabbed my face into her hands. "Look at you. So handsome."

"Something smells good!" I exclaimed and went straight for the stove to see what it was. I lifted the aluminum foil that was wrapped around the plate of fried chicken. I peeked inside the oven only to find a pan of macaroni and cheese with the cheese bubbling over the sides.

"I made your favorite dessert," she boasted.

"You didn't…" I turned to see her face; wanted to see if she was serious.

"Sweet potato pie."

"Gram, you are the bomb!" I said.

"Now go get cleaned up, son. Your father will be here soon, and I want the three of us to sit down and have dinner together."

"My dad will be here soon? Have you talked to him?" I asked.

"No, I haven't talked to him. But doesn't he get in from work around five or six?"

"Not usually, Gram. Sometimes he doesn't get in until around ten or eleven…sometimes later."

"Are you kidding me?" She looked mortified. "That won't work. It just won't work. That's unacceptable! When do the two of you spend time together?"

"Hmm…sometimes I'm still awake when he gets in, and he'll stick his head in and say goodnight. And sometimes we watch *SportsCenter* together."

"*SportsCenter.*" She said it with such disappointment. "I don't like that, Drew. I don't like that one bit! He needs to spend quality time with you. He's your father, and he's no better than your mother if you never get to see him."

"It's really not that serious, Gram. I'm not a little kid anymore, so I don't really require that much supervision."

"I didn't say you needed supervision. I said you need quality time!" she said. "I'm going to have a word with him when he gets in. Now go get cleaned up. You and I will have dinner together."

It wasn't a good time to tell my grandmother that I wasn't hungry. That I usually grabbed a slice or two of pizza every day at Manny's before making it home from school. I didn't want her to think that she'd fried chicken for nothing, so I left the kitchen; rushed upstairs and changed into a pair of sweats and an old T-shirt. I washed my face and hands. By the time I returned, Gram had set the table for two.

I rubbed my palms together. "It looks good. Can't wait to dig in."

I took a seat across from Gram. She said a prayer over the food and then fixed my plate.

"So what's going on with you, Drew? You like that new school?"

"I love it, Gram," I told her. "And guess what...I landed a role in a play already."

"No kidding. You were always so good at that...acting and pretending." She giggled. I wasn't sure if that was a compliment or not.

"Dad's not feeling my new gig, though," I said; forgot who I was talking to.

"Speak English to me, boy. I don't know all that slang."

"He's not happy with me going to a performing arts school. He wants me to play basketball. He thinks that act-ing is for sissies."

"Oh, he does, does he?" she said matter-of-factly. "He

must've forgotten that he was an actor himself back in the day."

"My dad was an actor?"

"And a wannabe musician," she said with a laugh. "He begged us to let him take acting classes. And so we did. But that only lasted a hot minute. Then he wanted to play the guitar. And we got him guitar lessons."

"Are you serious?" I was shocked. "My dad played the guitar?"

"He never told you?" she asked. "Skeeter was actually pretty good at it."

Skeeter was my dad's nickname. To have such a manly name like *Derrick Bishop,* and then to be called Skeeter instead—that had to be rough. When he was younger, he was so skinny—puny is what my grandmother called him—they compared him to a mosquito. Hence, Skeeter was born. I was glad I didn't have any whack nicknames like that.

"Nah, he never told me that, Gram. In fact, he was so mad when I told him that I wanted to audition for Premiere High. And he pretty much stopped talking to me when I got in."

"Are you kidding me? Why didn't you call me? I would've got into Skeeter's behind!"

Sometimes my grandmother forgot that my dad was a grown man and was too old to be scolded like a child. She claimed that he was never too old for her to whip his behind. And if I got out of line, she would whip mine, too. And up until about three years ago, she stood true to her word. She had given me plenty of whippings. She wasn't afraid to get a belt when one was needed. Soon I was too tall for her to handle. I'd stand there with my arms folded across my chest, refusing to cry with every swat. That only made her madder, and pretty soon she just stopped trying.

"I think he'll come around. He just needs time to let things marinate," I told her. "You should come to my performance next month, Gram…sit in the front row and be in my cheering section."

"I sure will, sweetie. You just let me know when the date is, and I'll be right there. Yes, I will."

"I love you, Gram. You take such good care of us."

"It's my job, baby."

It was true. She took great care of us. Without her, we'd fall apart, Dad and I. I would never have any clean underwear, and I wouldn't know what a good meal was. Beanies and weenies was not it. She gave us structure. She said that we gave her structure. After Granddad died of cancer, she said she needed someone to take care of—something to do that was worthwhile. Otherwise she'd crawl into a hole and die. Dad and I had a good life. It wasn't perfect, but it was healthy. But I was glad for Gram. She gave us the things that we were missing.

"Now, what about girls? The last time we talked, you were seeing some little girl…Brittany or Bridgette."

"Brianna."

"Yes, that's it. Are you still stringing her along?"

My grandmother was so straightforward. She never beat

around the bush, she just said it. Whatever was on her mind, she said it. I loved that about her. I respected that, because you never had to guess where you stood with her.

"I wasn't stringing her along, Gram. I just wasn't ready for a relationship like she was."

"Well, you should've just been up front with her. Let her know that you're still sowing your oats and you had no intention of settling down."

"Sowing my oats, Gram? Come on."

"Okay, what do you youngsters call it now? Getting busy...getting jiggy with it?

"You been watching *Fresh Prince of Bel-Air* again?" I asked with a laugh. "I just wanted to kick it with some other people for a while."

"Kick it! So, that's the new phrase. Thanks for keeping me up on the slang," she said with a giggle. "One of these days, Drew, some girl is going to come along...and she's gonna knock you off your feet. You won't know what hit you."

"I think she's already come along."

"Oh, really?"

"Yeah. Her name is Marisol Garcia. Mari for short."

"She's Hispanic."

"Yes. Very beautiful. Funny. Smart..."

"But..."

"But we're just good friends, and I like kicking it with her. We hang out, like buddies. Don't wanna mess that up.

But when I'm around her, I feel all these things and I don't know what to do about it. It's, like…confusing…"

"Why don't you just ask her out? I mean on a real date… and not just hang out. That way you can determine which you like better…hanging out or dating."

"I came pretty close to asking her to the fall social. It's this dance…a formal dance at school…sort of like home-coming at other schools."

"And? What happened?"

"I couldn't do it. I lost my nerve, and instead asked her if she would tutor me in algebra," I said. "Besides, I'm not even sure that I want to show up at a dance with a girl. I mean, the other girls will get the wrong idea. They might think I'm in an exclusive relationship or something, and I don't want that. I just wanna kick it for now."

She laughed heartily, as if I'd just told the funniest joke ever. I didn't understand the laughter; just patiently waited for her to get herself together.

"You really like her. I can tell," she finally said. "But I have to tell you, son…somebody else is gonna scoop her up right out from under you…while you're busy…*kicking it*. Don't wait too long to tell her how you feel."

"It's not that serious, Gram. It's just Mari. She's cool."

"Okay, sweetness. But remember that old saying, 'he who snoozes, loses,'" she said and grabbed another piece of fried chicken; set it on her plate. "Now, how about a game of poker after dinner?"

"What you want? You want some of this?" I asked my grandmother.

"I can't wait to spank your little behind, boy. Show you who is boss!" she boasted.

I ate quickly. A game of poker with my grandmother was like nothing else. It was the ultimate challenge. I got a rush just thinking about it. She definitely knew a lot about the game, and I'd been trying to beat her since I was five years old. One of my purposes in life was to beat Gram at one game of poker. I didn't know if it would ever happen, but it sure was fun trying.

"I'll get the cards."

sixteen

Marisol

WE stood onstage; our fingers intertwined as we held hands. I closed my eyes tightly and said a little prayer. I usually prayed only during Sunday morning Mass at my church, but today I needed an extra prayer. When I opened my eyes, I stared at the wooden floors beneath my Chuck Taylor sneakers. They were shiny floors, I thought. The school's janitor had done a pretty good job of buffing them the night before. In order to avoid looking out at the crowd, I glanced over at Jasmine's matching black Chuck Taylors. What were the odds that we owned sneakers that were almost identical? They went well with our black leggings.

"When I call your name, please step forward," stated the white-haired judge as she made notes on a notepad. "Belinda Lewis…"

Belinda Lewis hesitated for a moment then stepped forward.

"Audrey Harris…"

Audrey, who stood next to me, left my side and stepped forward.

"Michael Thomas," the judge called, and Michael stepped forward.

Three names had been called, and there were two names left. A total of five people were to be finalists. The five people who were chosen by the judges today would be Hollywood-bound. My knees shook as I listened for the last two names to be called.

"Jordan Felton."

My heart dropped. With one name left, I knew that one of us—Jasmine or I—wasn't going. We squeezed each other's hand tighter as we listened for the final name to be called. One of us had to make it; we just had to.

"Alisha Coleman."

Alisha Coleman? Seriously? She'd stumbled over her own feet during her routine. How could the very last name be Alisha Coleman? Both Jasmine and I could dance circles around Alisha Coleman. I was disappointed, and I struggled to fight back the tears. I started going over our routine in my head; wondered what we could've done better. The judge's voice snapped me out of my trance.

"Those of you who have stepped forward, you are all wonderfully talented dancers. However, I'm sorry to inform you that you are not this year's finalists. Thank you for entering the competition, and I encourage you to give it another try next year…"

What?

"…if you would, please exit the stage to your left…"

Did I hear her correctly?

"...the five of you remaining, please take a bow. You should be very proud of yourselves. You are Dance America's final five, and you will be going to Hollywood to compete for the role in a feature film that is currently being produced. The winner will also receive a scholarship in the amount of five thousand dollars toward your college education. Good luck to you all in Los Angeles."

I couldn't contain my excitement, and neither could Jasmine, because we both started jumping and screaming at the same time. This had to be the most exciting day in the lives of five teenagers. The five of us, who barely even knew each other, started hugging and crying. It was an emotional moment.

Once my heart stopped beating so fast, and reality finally set in, I looked out at the crowd. I caught the eye of my father, who was standing and holding on to my mother. She was crying, and although he tried to hide it, he also had a tear in his eye. They were proud of me. I knew it the moment I saw them. My brother, Nico, gave me a thumbs-up, and I gave him a smile. It was definitely a proud day for the Garcia family.

As I stepped inside the doorway, someone threw rice in my hair. Everyone started cheering. Grace hugged me, and Kristina started rambling in Spanish about how proud she was to be my friend. It seemed as if the entire neighborhood had gathered in our small living room. With balloons and banners all over the room, it was clearly a celebration party, especially for me.

"I am so proud of you, Chica!" said Grace.

"Me, too," Kristina said.

I scanned the crowd. "Is Luz here?" I asked.

Grace looked at Kristina, and Kristina looked at me; shook her head no. I was disappointed. Somehow, when I thought of all of my friends and neighbors gathering in one place, I expected to see Luz. Her parents were there, and so was her younger sister. It seemed awkward that she didn't even feel the need to show up.

"She'll come around, Mari," said Grace. "Just give her time."

"I think her mom said she had the flu or something," Kristina added.

"It's okay. At least you guys are here, right?" I asked, not really expecting a response. Then I yelled, "I'm going to Hollywood!"

The three of us screamed.

It was all so surreal.

That night as I lay in my bed, staring at the ceiling, I went over the day's events in my head. Becoming one of Dance America's top five had been the single most exciting thing that had ever happened to me. I was sure of it. I didn't know if I would be able to sleep through the night. I had homework to complete, but how could I do homework when so many wonderful things were racing through my head? There were so many things to do before heading to Hollywood in a couple of weeks. I closed my eyes as tight as I could. In a matter of one day, my entire life had changed.

seventeen

Marisol

strolling through the hallways of Premiere was different than it had been before. This time as we strolled, Jasmine and I were celebrities, and suddenly everyone knew us by name—quite an accomplishment for a freshmen and sophomore who would never have been recognized otherwise.

I took a seat in my usual spot at the back of the classroom. It was always a joy to see Jesse Lucas walk into the room. With his brown curly locks and light brown eyes, he was one of the best-looking guys at Premiere. He wore a tight shirt that hugged his muscular frame with an argyle sweater vest on top and a pair of slim black jeans tucked inside his sneakers. His smile was like the sunshine that crept through the window in my room on a Saturday morning. And he smelled so good—like the men's fragrance counter at Bloomingdale's.

"Hey," he said and then smiled; took a seat in front of me.

I took a look behind me to see who he was talking to.

Surely he wasn't talking to me. I didn't exist in Jesse Lucas's world. There was no one behind me, so I took a chance that he was talking to me.

"Hey," I replied and smiled.

He usually plopped down in his seat and never even turned around. I would spend the entire hour looking at the back of his beautiful head. But today, I wasn't invisible.

"Congrats on winning Dance America. You were pretty good out there," he said.

Was he actually having a conversation with me?

"Thanks," I told him.

He unzipped his backpack and took out his American history book, slammed it onto his desk. I watched as he pulled out a spiral notebook and a mechanical pencil.

He turned around in his seat again and whispered, "You're going to the fall social, right?"

"Umm...yes. Planning to," I said.

"Already have a date?" he asked.

"Umm...not really. Actually...no, I don't." Why was I stumbling over my words? He was just a boy.

"Would you like to go with me?" he asked.

I was speechless. My mind went blank. I thought he asked if I would like to go with him. Underneath my desk, I pinched my leg, just to make sure I wasn't dreaming. Was this his idea of a practical joke? I watched his face; wanted to see if he was serious or not. First of all, girls like me didn't get asked to the fall social by boys like Jesse Lucas— the most handsome boy in school.

"Umm…I guess so," I told him; wanted to remain calm. Wanted him to think that it was no big deal that he asked.

I wondered if I sounded stupid or immature, but what could I say? He'd caught me off guard. What gave him the right to just pop into my American history class and ask me to the dance? Who did he think he was anyway?

"I'm Jesse, by the way." He held his hand out for a shake.

I know who you are, dude! The entire female student body knows who you are!

I grabbed his hand; pretended not to know his name.

"Nice to meet you, Jesse. I'm Marisol."

"I know who you are." He smiled that sunshinelike smile. "Where do you live?"

Was he coming over for a visit? Why did he need to know where I lived?

"I live in Sunset Park," I told him.

"Brooklyn." He nodded his head; jotted something down on a piece of notebook paper; ripped it in half and handed it to me. He'd scribbled his name and phone number on the page. "When you call me, we can talk about what we're wearing."

He *was* serious. It wasn't a practical joke. Of all the pretty girls at Premiere High, Jesse Lucas was asking me to the fall social.

"Okay." I gnawed on my number two pencil. Needed to get rid of my nervous energy.

Jesse turned around in his seat; opened his textbook to the page we were studying. That was the end of the conversation. I opened my book also; pondered on the thought of the hottest boy in school asking me to the fall social. I wondered how my parents would react to him picking me up at my house. So many thoughts were rushing through my head at a rapid pace. I needed to focus on history, but who could focus at a time like this?

The dismissal bell snapped me back to reality. I sat there for a moment staring at my spiral notebook and the blank page. I hadn't taken a single note. Jesse grinned as he gathered his things and exited the room.

As I walked toward the door, Mr. McKinney stopped me.

"Marisol, may I see you for a moment?" he asked.

"Yeah, sure," I said and made my way to his desk.

"Um, I graded your American history exam—" he handed it to me "—and it's not good."

I stared at the large red mark at the top of the exam. A big fat D+ was plastered across the page. In all my years, I'd never received a D on any homework assignment or exam. My heart sank.

"Wow," I said under my breath.

"I don't really know what happened, but your overall grade sort of plummeted from an A+ to a very low C pretty quickly. I don't know if you're having trouble at home, but if you need some assistance, I'd be happy to meet with you after school this Friday afternoon and try to figure out how to bring that grade back up."

"I can't on Friday." Friday was the day I was scheduled

to leave for Hollywood. I wouldn't be at school on Friday, but I wanted to at least find out how to bring my grade up. "Can we do it today or tomorrow?"

"I'm sorry, Marisol. The only day I have available is Friday afternoon. I was hoping to give you an opportunity to retake your exam that day. If you score a higher grade on the exam, we can get your grade up to at least a B."

I stood there. I was between a rock and a hard place. Grades were definitely important, but so was Dance America. I wanted to make the right decision. I hadn't failed the exam. A D+ was a passing grade. And my overall grade in the class was a C. If I worked really hard after my return from California, I was sure that I could improve my grade. It was still early in the year. I had time, and I had no choice. My parents would have a fit if I failed any of my classes.

In the hallway, I grabbed Jasmine by the arm; pulled her through the crowd.

"You will never believe who asked me to the dance," I told her.

"Drew Bishop," she said matter-of-factly.

"No."

"Hmm…not Drew?" She was surprised. "Then who?"

"Jesse Lucas," I said and grinned; stood in front of her.

"Beautiful Jesse Lucas, with the curly brown hair, tight abs and drop-dead-gorgeous smile?" she asked.

"Don't forget the light brown eyes and muscular arms," I told her.

"Oh, my God, you're serious!"

"Totally…serious."

"What did you say?"

"I said yes! Maybe I should've said no at first…you know, played hard to get." I pondered it for the first time. What seemed like the best option at first suddenly seemed silly. Was I too anxious? "I should've played hard to get."

"You did the right thing. He's so cute," she said, "and it's just a dance. You're not marrying the guy."

"True."

As we stepped out into the breezy fall air, I zipped my jacket up and adjusted my bag on my shoulder. "What about Drew? I told him I was going stag," I said. Although Drew wasn't my boyfriend, I still felt somewhat of an allegiance to him.

"What *about* Drew? He had his chance to ask you to the dance, and he didn't. It's his loss, right?"

"Yeah. I guess you're right."

"We can't sit around waiting for guys to ask us to the dance, Mari. I mean, look at us! We're celebrities now." She giggled and started dancing down Madison Avenue toward the subway station. "Guys want to date us, and girls want to be us!"

She slipped a cigarette from its package—her afternoon ritual; lit it. She was right. I was a celebrity now, and it was time I started behaving like one. Winning the Dance America competition had changed my life—and hers. All of our dreams were about to come true. Although I didn't feel much like a celebrity when I stepped onto the train and slipped into the seat next to the drunken guy with the body odor. That was enough to snap me back to reality.

I recognized the smell of my mother's paella—the spices and tomatoes hit my nose the minute I walked through the door. Walking through the front door of my house felt different today. I wasn't the same Mari anymore—I was different. I couldn't wait to glance at my reflection in the mirror just to see if I had changed.

"Hola, novio," said Mami as she talked to someone on the phone.

"Hola, Mami." I dropped my bag in the middle of the floor.

"Take your bag to your room, Mari," she said, "and tell your brother to come here. I need for him to put these boxes near the front door. Things we're giving away to charity."

I glanced over at the boxes in question. Inside one of the boxes was my favorite sweater. It was worn, and there was a hole underneath the armpit where the seam was loose, and there was a permanent stain on the collar, but I loved that sweater. I grabbed it from the box; held it in the air. "You're giving away my purple sweater?"

"I haven't seen you wear that sweater in at least a year, Mari."

"But it's mine. And I love it," I pleaded.

"Mari, the things in these boxes are for charity…for

someone less fortunate. You've enjoyed the sweater for a long time. Now it's time to give to those who don't have anything."

"I thought we gave stuff away that we didn't want anymore," I said, "not stuff that we still wear and love!"

"Mari, you're being very selfish. You got three new sweaters for Christmas last year," Mami said. "You can't be blessed until you bless others."

"Fine, Mami. Why don't you give away the new sweaters, too? I got a new pair of skinny jeans last week that I bought with my allowance. Maybe I can give those away, too."

"Mari, I don't like your attitude."

She was right. I was being a brat. And what did it matter what she gave away anyway? I was a celebrity, and soon I'd be able to buy a thousand sweaters, and a thousand pairs of jeans. I wouldn't need to give away my hand-me-downs to those who are less fortunate. I could buy them all new stuff.

"Sorry, Mami. I was being selfish," I said. I tossed the sweater back into the box.

She gave me a strange look. She probably wanted to check my forehead for a fever, but she didn't. Instead she went back to her telephone conversation.

I headed upstairs to my brother's room.

Nico's door was shut and his music was loud. I tapped on the door—lightly at first. When there was no answer, I knocked louder. Still, no response. I turned the knob on the door and peeked inside. Nico's clothes were laid out on the bed; a pair of freshly ironed jeans, socks, underwear and a crisp white shirt. His books were scattered all over the floor, along with tons of CDs. Candy wrappers and soda cans were thrown everywhere. His room was a mess.

I tiptoed inside; just to pry. My brother had become so secretive lately, and I wanted to see what was going on in his life. In the past, we'd been so close. I could talk to him about everything, and he shared everything with me also. Besides Luz, Nico had always been my best friend. I could talk to him about boys and he would give me advice. Nico had one steady girlfriend in his life since fifth grade. Gabriela. They were destined to be together—completely made for each other. That is until Gabriela went away to Connecticut to spend the summer with her dad. When she came back, she was different. New hairdo. New wardrobe. New boyfriend. Nico was devastated. He confided in me that he no longer wanted to live. He'd rather die than live without Gabriela. I was worried, but I figured he'd get over it in time. That was six months ago, and the more time passed, the more Nico became stranger by the day.

He would hit on my friends and try to seem like a normal teenage boy, but behind those deep brown eyes, I could see his pain. I became more concerned when I saw him hanging out occasionally with Diego and his posse. We all knew that Diego was bad news and was no one that Nico needed to share company with.

I started sorting through the mess on his bed. I wasn't

quite sure what I was looking for. I guess I just needed a clue as to where my brother's head was—what secrets he had hidden behind his strange behavior. Underneath the sports section of the newspaper sprawled across the bed, I spotted the silver piece of metal with the black handle. A gun. My heart started pounding when I saw it. I stood there. Paralyzed.

"What are you doing in here?" Nico asked, with wet hair and a towel wrapped around his waist.

I picked up the gun, turned toward Nico and waved it in the air. "What are you doing with this, Nico?"

He snatched it; tossed it on the bed. "None of your business. Why are you even in here?"

"What's going on with you, Nico?" I lowered my voice. "Why are you having words with Diego in the middle of the street? And why are you carrying a gun?"

"It's my business, Marisol. Stay out of it."

"It is my business. If my brother is carrying a gun then it's my business." I missed my brother. I missed the Nico who would share everything with me. "Maybe Mami and Poppy would like to know that you have a shotgun in their house."

"It's not a shotgun. It's a Magnum .357. And you wouldn't tell them."

"I would."

"You'd better not." Nico grabbed my arm, squeezed it tight. "Do you hear me, Mari? You'd better not breathe a word to them about this."

The grip on my arm became tighter.

"You're hurting me," I told him.

With fear and anger in his voice, and through clenched teeth, he said, "Promise you won't say anything."

"Nico, you're hurting me."

He squeezed tighter. "Promise!"

"I promise," I said. I wanted him to let go. Tears were threatening to fall from my eyes.

I saw something in my brother's eyes that I'd never seen before. He was different; not the same loving Nico who used to protect me.

"Why are you shutting me out, Nico? You were my best friend once..."

"You have to go, Mari, so I can get dressed." He held on to the towel that was wrapped around his waist; walked over to the door and opened it wider.

I walked out of his room.

"Mami wants to see you downstairs," I told him.

"Yeah," he said and then slammed his door shut.

He was up to no good, and I knew it.

eighteen

Drew

"...and Kobe Bryant comes down the court at full speed, the ball in his hand. He's recovered from an injury to his right knee. He's completely healed, and completely out of control. The crowd is going crazy. He's so hot, he's on fire...LeBron James is under the goal, with his hands in the air..."

"I don't wanna be LeBron James. I wanna be Lamar what's-his-name," Mari said and giggled. "You know, Khloe Kardashian's husband, Lamar. The tall black guy with the bald head."

I stopped in midstream; stopped bouncing the imaginary ball—a pair of dress socks. "You can't be Lamar Odom. He's on the same team as Kobe. You gotta be somebody else. Someone who plays for the Miami Heat. Somebody like LeBron James or Dwayne Wade."

"Can I be Shaq?" she asked.

"Shaq plays for Boston, Mari," I said with a laugh. "And besides, you're way too pretty to be Shaq. How about Carlos Arroyo? He's a Hispanic dude."

"Is he cute?"

"I don't know if he's cute, Mari. He's a pretty good player."

"Okay, I'll be him." Mari held her hands high in the air; her best attempt at defense.

I dribbled around her, faked her out and then dunked the socks into the trash can. I did the Dougie—a dance created by rap artist Doug E. Fresh.

Mari picked up the socks; took them out of bounds, which was on the other side of my bed. Dressed in a pair of my boxer shorts and my white dress shirt, she pretended to dribble the ball as she slid across our hardwood floors. She looked cute wearing my oversize clothes, and she didn't seem uncomfortable about it, either.

After school, I'd convinced her to tutor me at my apartment instead of Starbucks or at Manny's. I was anxious to show her my trophies—all the trophies that I'd won over the course of my basketball career since junior high school. We studied algebra at my dining room table. She was so smart, and the subject came so easy for her. I envied her; wished I could catch on so quickly, but I'd missed out on so much being a jock.

When I accidentally knocked over Mari's glass of Wild Purple Smash Hawaiian Punch, it splattered all over her white blouse and khaki pants. After apologizing until I was blue in the face, I offered her one of my dress shirts and a pair of my boxer shorts—the new ones with the purple and yellow stripes. She was hesitant at first but then crept into the guest bathroom and changed. When she came out, I couldn't take my eyes off her. It was weird, but my shirt made her look so much more attractive. I grabbed my Yankees cap, placed it backward on her head. I loved a girl in a baseball cap. After that, somehow we ended up playing a game of sock basketball.

"I can't stay long," she reminded me as we both collapsed on the bed. "I have to get home soon."

"Okay, as soon as your clothes are done, I'll walk you to the subway."

I escorted her into the family room; turned on my dad's old stereo—the one that he'd found at a rummage sale one Saturday afternoon. It was his pride and joy. He loved the fact that he could play his old albums and records on it. His albums were so different than my collection of CDs. They looked ancient, but I was interested in them. The first time he showed me how to play one on his turntable, I watched it spin around in a circle; it was fascinating. Sometimes when he wasn't home, I'd listen to his old music—rappers like Doug E. Fresh, Eric B. and Rakim, and Grandmaster Flash and the Furious Five. Some of their stuff was corny at first, but eventually it grew on me. Now it was the music that I preferred.

I placed my dad's Grandmaster Flash album on the turntable, turned up the volume on the stereo.

"What's that?" Mari asked.

"Grandmaster Flash." I handed her the album cover.

She stared at the picture of guys wearing Kangol hats

and carrying around a huge boom box. She laughed as she handed it back to me.

"It's my dad's old stuff," I explained.

"It sounds like some music that Jasmine's dad played when he taught us how to pop-lock for the dance contest." She laughed and then gave me a demonstration; started pop-locking.

I followed suit and soon we were both pop-locking— almost challenging each other. She showed me her moves, and I showed her what I had. I had to admit, she was a great dancer. I wasn't surprised that she was a finalist in this year's Dance America contest. She deserved it.

After becoming bored with dancing, we decided on another game of one-on-one while her clothes dried. This time with a real basketball. She didn't know very much about basketball, so I had to give her a crash course. She could barely bounce the basketball at first, but eventually she picked it up. I couldn't help but laugh as she dribbled with two hands at first, and double dribbled a few times.

"Okay, so let's see your jump shot," I told Mari. "If you're gonna be Arroyo, you gotta have a nice outside jump shot."

She gave her jump shot a try, but it was bad—terrible even, but I hid my laughter. Didn't want to embarrass her. I was enjoying her company and wanted to prolong her visit as much as possible. She managed to get the ball back in her possession, attempted to dribble and went up for a shot. I don't know what came over me, but I grabbed her by the waist; gave her a tight squeeze. Her arms suddenly wrapped themselves around my neck and I took in her smell. I could feel my heart pounding as I glanced at her lips. They were purple from the Wild Purple Smash Hawaiian Punch. I wanted to kiss them. Just as my lips were headed toward hers, my cell phone buzzed. I let go of Mari's waist; pulled the phone out of the pocket of my basketball shorts; looked at the screen. Preston. His timing was terrible.

"I'd better go...um...check on my clothes," Mari said and headed for our laundry room as if she already knew her way around. She came back with her dried clothes in her hand; stepped into the guest bathroom to change.

I turned off the stereo and grabbed the television remote control; flipped to ESPN. Relaxing on the sofa in the living room, I caught a glimpse of *SportsCenter* while Mari changed back into her school clothes. I wondered what would've happened if Preston hadn't interrupted.

When she stepped out of the bathroom fully dressed, I looked at her face. Hoped I hadn't scared her too bad. I wanted to know what it was like to kiss her, but I knew that the moment had slipped away. To go back would be awkward.

There was an uncomfortable silence in the air as I walked Mari to the subway station. I knew that I had to break the tension; otherwise we'd never be the same.

"You really suck at basketball," I told her. "You really have a lot to learn."

"Well, thank you very much," she said with a smile.

"You're a pretty good dancer though. I can't believe you can pop-lock like that. You're almost as good as me."

"Almost as good?"

"You got a lot to learn, kid. About basketball, and about pop-locking," I told her.

"And I guess you're going to teach me."

"Thought you'd never ask," I said. "Tomorrow after school...same time, same place?"

As we stood in front of the subway station, I stared at Mari; waiting for her answer.

"Okay, I guess I'll see you tomorrow then."

"I guess so," I said. "Text me when you get home."

"I'll think about it." She giggled and then headed into the station; never looked back.

My heart was doing weird things as I watched her leave. I didn't know what it meant, so I ignored it. It was probably just heartburn.

nineteen

Marisol

Dressed in a gray suit and gray high heels, J.C. introduced one of the producers for Dance America. He was the epitome of Hollywood with a pair of mirrored sunglasses on top of his head. Wearing a silk white shirt and a pair of expensive slacks, he explained in detail what would take place in Los Angeles. The final Dance America contestants and our parents sat around a table in one of the school's conference rooms. I watched as my parents carefully read over every single detail of my contract. They had so many questions for the producer—so many comments. Way more than the other parents. I thought that they'd never sign the contract and give the green light for me to go to Hollywood. But eventually, they were satisfied. And with a blue ballpoint pen, my father carefully signed each page.

My heart danced as I watched my mother's face soften a little. She was starting to feel more comfortable with J.C. and finally realized that she'd have to ease up a little. And although the producer seemed a bit superficial at first, he showed true concern for my mother's feelings when she expressed them. With my mother feeling better about the trip, I became excited. I glanced over at Jasmine, who sat next to her father. He had a few questions of his own, but he also seemed satisfied with the details as he signed her contract. Jasmine gave me a smile and a thumbs-up.

As I watched the black town car with the tinted windows pull up next to the curb, I remembered thinking this day would never come. My bags stood next to the door—an upright black suitcase on wheels and a small, bright yellow duffel bag with a broken zipper. The yellow duffel bag was stuffed with makeup and hair products that I would need for the weekend in Hollywood.

"Mari, your ride is here," Mami called from downstairs.

The Dance America competition had sent a chauffer-driven town car to pick up all the contestants at their homes. I'd been looking out my bedroom window for the past two hours, waiting for the car to pull up. Too excited to eat the breakfast that Mami had prepared for me. Who could eat at a time like this?

"On my way!" I yelled to her.

I gave myself another glance in the mirror; checked my hair and my makeup. All was well. I grabbed a jacket as my dad stepped into the room.

"Is your bag ready?" he asked and grabbed the handle of my suitcase.

"Yeah." I took a deep breath.

"You ready?" he asked.

"I think so," I said.

I followed Poppy down the stairs as we met the driver at the front door. Poppy handed the slender man my suitcase, and I held on tightly to my makeup bag. Mami stood there with tears in her eyes.

"I guess this is it, huh?" I asked.

"I'm so proud of you, Marisol. But I feel like you're going away forever."

"It's just for a few days, Mami. I'll be back on Sunday. Unless I win the competition. Then I'll be back next Wednesday."

"And you packed everything, *sí?*" she asked.

"*Sí,* Mami. Everything."

"Shower gel, lotion, toothpaste, clean underwear?"

"*Sí,* Mami!" I said. "You're worrying too much."

"This is hard for me, Mari. You've never been outside of New York or Jersey."

"I know, Mami, but I'll be fine." I gave her a kiss on the cheek and then kissed my dad. "I'll see you in a few days."

"Don't forget to hide your ugly face, so they won't think that you're a terrorist." Nico sat at the top of the stairs in a pair of pajama pants and an old T-shirt. He wiped sleep from his eyes.

I gave him a grin; quickly walked up the stairs and gave my brother a kiss on the cheek. "See ya, stupid."

"You should go, *bebé,*" Poppy said. "Don't want to miss your flight."

I stepped out into the cool air, zipped my jacket and headed for the Lincoln town car. My friends and neighbors had gathered.

"We love you, Mari," said Mrs. Vasquez from two houses down.

"Make us proud!" someone yelled.

"Send me a text the minute you get to Cali, Chica!" yelled Kristina.

"Me, too," Grace said, and they both gave me a big hug.

I stepped into the backseat of the car as the driver held the door open for me. I smiled as we slowly pulled away from the curb. It was all so surreal.

Waiting for my flight to board, I sat slouched in my seat at LaGuardia Airport. I wondered where Jasmine was. Our flight was due to board at any moment, and there was no sign of her. I pulled my cell phone out and sent her another text message.

Where RU? Boarding soon.

Can't go, Mari. My dad had a heart attack.

What? OMG!

I'm scared.

I'm so sorry! What about Dance America?

They sent someone else in my place.

Who?

I dunno. Wildcard contestant.

I can't do this without you.

Yes U can. U don't need me.

Be strong Jazz.
I will. U too.

I was numb. The news of Jasmine's father had me thrown off. So many thoughts raced through my head. I hoped that Jasmine's dad would pull through, and I softly said a little prayer for him. I thought of my own father. Poppy. And how I would feel if he had a heart attack. I would be scared, too. Then I thought of Dance America. It wouldn't be the same without Jasmine. We'd started this thing together, and won it—*together.* Everything would be different without her.

I looked at my watch as the attendant announced that we would begin boarding in ten minutes. As I glanced toward the ticket counter, I noticed a familiar face. Luz stood there; a carry-on bag draped across her shoulder and her fingers wrapped around a cup from Starbucks. She wore a white bubble coat—the one with the fur around the hood. I recognized it because it was my coat. I'd let her borrow it last winter and she never returned it. And the jeans I had on belonged to her. It wasn't unusual for us to swap clothing. That's what best friends did.

I needed to know why Luz was at LaGuardia Airport, in the same boarding area; waiting for the same flight. I stood and headed her way.

"Hey," I said to her.

She didn't look surprised to see me. She just took a sip from her cup and said, "Hey."

"What are you doing here?"

"I'm going to California," she said.

"Really?"

"Yeah. Dance America called me up, said that one of the contestants had an emergency family issue, and they needed someone to go in her place," she said.

"Jasmine." I whispered it; sort of to myself. "Wow, so you were the wildcard contestant."

"Yeah, I guess so."

"Well, I'm glad. If I had to go with anybody, Luz, it would be you," I told her. I really meant it.

"You mean that?" she asked. Surprised.

"Of course. You are my best friend."

"I thought Jasmine was your new best friend."

"I like Jasmine. She's cool," I explained, "and yes, she's my friend, but you and I have history."

"I thought you had tossed me aside."

"I thought you'd tossed me aside," I said. "It was like you hated me or something."

"I don't hate you, Mari. I felt hurt and kind of left out when you and Jasmine started dancing together. It was like, you and I had decided to dance together, and suddenly I was, like, the third wheel."

"It wasn't even like that," I explained. "I know that we both thought a bunch of things that were wrong, Luz. Can we just start over?"

She took another sip from her cup. It was as if she was giving my comment some thought.

"Okay, yeah. We can start over, Chica," she finally said and then smiled.

I gave my friend a hug, right there in the midst of the crowd of passengers waiting for our flight. They simply watched; giving us strange looks as we embraced. I didn't care. I had my friend back, and that was all that mattered.

As we drove down Hollywood Boulevard, we breathed in the fresh California air. Our windows were rolled all the way down as we sat on the edges of our seats in the back of the town car. The palm trees were beautiful. Los Angeles was way different from our home in Brooklyn. In Brooklyn, there was nothing pretty to see—only smog and garbage. But in Los Angeles, the streets were clean, the grass was green and you could breathe in the fresh air.

There weren't any cab drivers yelling profanity out the windows of their cars. Instead, there were people jogging along the sidewalks and people walking their dogs. There were strange people strolling down Hollywood Boule-vard—such as the transvestite wearing a bleach-blond wig, a tight-fitting dress and hot-pink stilettos. I looked over at Luz to see if she'd seen it, too. With raised eyebrows, we both giggled at the same time. We were used to seeing strange people in New York, but this was a different sort of strange.

The driver of our car was listening to Gnarls Barkley's "Crazy" on his radio. Our excitement got the best of us and we started singing along with the song.

"Can you turn that up, please?" Luz asked. I couldn't believe she'd asked that.

The blond-haired man caught a glimpse of us in his rear-view mirror before turning up the volume on the radio. We started dancing in our seats. It felt so good to be in L.A. It was as if we'd traveled to another world. After the long flight from New York, it felt that way, too. It was exciting to be in another part of the country—to see a place that I'd only seen on television. I'd often dreamed of what California was like when I watched shows like *90210* and MTV's reality show *The Hills*. It was interesting to see how kids my age lived in California.

All I knew was New York. I'd never been outside New York or New Jersey and had never even flown before. It was all so new to me that it was hard to sit still in my seat. I wanted to scream at the top of my lungs and stick my head out the window; let the wind blow through my hair. As we drove down Wilshire Boulevard, I wondered how many stars we'd spot before we made it to our Beverly Hills hotel. Luz and I were speechless as we took in the breathtaking sights of the city. I was glad that we got to experience it together.

The car pulled into the circular drive of our hotel, and Luz and I stepped out of the car. The driver lifted our bags out of the trunk and set them on the ground. A red-haired woman with a spiked haircut rushed toward us carrying a clipboard.

"You must be Marisol Garcia and Luz Hernandez," she announced.

"Yes," we said in unison.

"Welcome to Los Angeles. I'm Gloria, your chaperone. I am here to make sure you have everything that you need to make your trip fabulous," she said and smiled. "Now, follow me. I'll show you to your room."

We were silent as we followed Gloria to the mirrored elevators.

"Congratulations, by the way," Gloria said. "You both should be very proud."

"Thank you," I said.

"Are you hungry?" she asked.

"Very," I answered for Luz and me. It suddenly dawned on me that I'd missed breakfast, and in that instant, my stomach started making all sorts of grumbling noises. It was as if it heard my conversation.

"Okay, great. Once we get you settled into your room, we'll trample over to the Hard Rock Cafe for burgers. How's that?"

Fantastic! I wanted to yell, but instead I said, "Cool."

With our backs against the wall of the elevator, Luz and I grabbed each other's hand and squeezed tight. It was our way of screaming without actually screaming. We didn't want Gloria to think that we'd lost our minds.

The suite was massive, with two separate bedrooms, a full-size kitchen and a sofa and love seat in the living room. I thought I'd died and gone to heaven. I wondered when the rest of the contestants would arrive and if we got first dibs on the bedrooms.

"You can toss a coin for whichever bedroom you want. April and Tiana, the other two female contestants, are right next door. And Todd, the male contestant, is right down the hall. A special dinner has been planned for you this evening. You will be dining with the producers of the film. Some of the actors will be there, too. Justin may even make an appearance…"

Did she say Justin might show up? This was way too much—too soon. I wasn't expecting to see Justin until tomorrow. My hair was a mess, and I hadn't packed a fabulous dinner outfit.

"…and after that, a very hot party has been planned in your honor at a local teen club." She walked over to the picture window and opened the blinds. "I urge you to get a good night's sleep tonight, because tomorrow morning, we're on location at Universal Studios, where you will dance for the producers and one of you will be selected to star in the film."

Everything was happening so fast, my head was beginning to spin. I was still stuck on the fact that this breathtaking room belonged to Luz and me alone. It was almost the size of our home in Sunset Park. And then the thought of having dinner with film producers and actors, and possibly Justin Bieber, blew my mind. And to think that in the morning, I would be stepping into a real live movie studio. I couldn't wait for Gloria to leave, so that I could release all the anxiety that I had bottled up inside me. I imagined that Luz was feeling the same way.

"Okay, ladies, I'm going to leave you alone to get freshened up. I'll meet you in the lobby in thirty minutes, and we'll head over to the Hard Rock Cafe for a bite to eat. That sound good?"

"Yes," we both said.

"Very well." Gloria walked to the door; opened it. "Then I'll see you both in a little bit."

She left, and the door slammed behind her.

"Oh, my God…oh, my God!" I yelled.

"I don't believe this!" yelled Luz, as she ran into one of the bedrooms; fell backward onto the bed. "I think I've died and gone to heaven."

"Me, too!" I yelled from the living room. "Can you believe this is our room and we don't have to share it with anybody else?"

"Can you believe that we're going to Universal Studios tomorrow?" She walked back into the living room and over to the window.

"We're stars!" I yelled at the top of my lungs and then softened my voice. "I'm so glad that I get to share this moment with you, Luz."

"Me too, Mari," she said, and then she hugged me. "Now, if you'll excuse me, I have to go take a shower. I have an appointment in thirty minutes."

We both laughed. Today, life had dealt us both a great hand.

twenty

Drew

It was probably true what they said—out of sight, out of mind. I'd been texting Mari all day and she hadn't responded to one single text. I missed her already, and she hadn't even been gone twenty-four hours. Before Mari left, she told Jasmine, who told Preston, who told me that Mari had a date for the fall social. Apparently she was going with Jesse Lucas, who was one of the most popular guys at Premiere. He played the saxophone and the drums, and I heard that he could even sing a little bit. I had to admit, I was a little jealous, but I held it together. Didn't want Jasmine or Preston to see me sweat. But Preston knew me better than anyone.

"Sorry that you had to find out this way, bro," said Preston.

"It's cool. I'm not even worried about it."

"I know in your heart, you wanted to ask her," he'd said.

"Nah, it was just…you know…I didn't want her to have to go stag," I lied.

Despite what I said, it had been my intent to ask Mari

to the dance, but I took for granted that she would still be available. I just assumed that she would go stag with Jasmine, and I'd meet her there. Since it was her first year at Premiere, I figured that nobody else would ask her—after all, she didn't know anyone.

I missed Mari, but I decided not to focus on her too much; I was becoming too attached, too clingy. After all, she was just a girl. And just a friend—as Preston and I were friends. Instead, I focused on my upcoming algebra exam. Acing that exam was the priority at hand. Nothing else was more important.

I had all weekend to study, so in the meantime, I grabbed Preston and the two of us headed to Central Park for a game of hoops with my old teammates. We'd finally squashed our differences about me leaving the team and they'd convinced me that just because I was pursuing my dream of acting, I shouldn't give up on the second-best thing in my life—basketball. They were right. I was so busy trying to prove a point—that I was more than just a baller—that I had forgotten that I had a strong love for the game. Basketball was like an old flame that refused to die. I still wanted it; just not full time.

I walked up, with my ball in hand—bouncing it and dribbling it between my legs. Preston took a seat on the bleachers. He was there just to observe.

"What y'all want?" I asked with a wide grin on my face.

My friends had missed me. I could tell by the way they gathered around me and started talking trash.

"Well, well, well. Look who decided to show up!" said Andre.

Andre had been my friend since elementary school. Besides Preston, he was one of my best friends and definitely a confidant. We'd played youth leagues together—baseball, basketball and soccer. I'd spent numerous nights at his house, and he at mine. I couldn't count the number of times we'd gotten in trouble together. Mostly he got in trouble—I just happened to be at the wrong place at the wrong time.

"It's Drew somebody...I can't remember his last name," Kev teased and everybody laughed.

"Just take the ball out, fool!" I yelled and tossed the ball into Kev's chest.

"Oh, he wants to play," Antwoine stated. "You mean you still got game?"

"More game than your mama." I played the dozens.

It wasn't unusual for us to talk about each other's mothers. It was what we did. We talked junk on the court. But I had the utmost respect for Mrs. Neal, Antwoine's mom, and our heckling was done all in fun.

"Okay, let's make sure that corny school hasn't turned you into a sissy," said Andre. "Who you want on your team?"

"I'll take Kev," I said, and nobody was surprised. Kev was big—at least six foot three. He was our team's center and he was great at defense.

Andre looked around the court. "I'll take Antwoine and Jay."

"Okay, well, give me Oscar, Dave and…"

"Pick me, Drew," said Malik, the smallest guy at the park that day.

Malik was a little, annoying kid who used to follow me around the neighborhood. He was my protégé. He was in the eighth grade and usually just sat on the sidelines and watched as the older guys played. But I'd heard that he had game this year, and that he'd even grown an inch taller.

"I'll take Malik." I wasn't sure what I was doing except giving a deserving kid a chance, as somebody did for me when I was his age. Besides, it was just a game.

"Malik?" Andre and Jay asked in unison.

"He's little, but he's quick. And what do you care anyway?"

"Do your thing, bro," Andre said and then picked his final two players.

Malik took the ball out of bounds and the game was on. It felt good running up and down that court, the soles of my sneakers hitting the pavement as I took the ball up in a layup. When the wind hit my lungs, I realized that I was out of shape. In just a few months, I'd gone from playing ball every day of my life to not playing at all. I had become lazy, and I was paying for it now as the rhythm of my breathing increased with every step. I faked it, though. Couldn't let them see me sweat. I had to bring my best game; otherwise, they would never let me live it down.

As the sun went down and I shot the last three-pointer, I glanced over at the bleachers. Preston was having a conversation with some guy dressed in a navy blazer and a blue-and-gray cap on his head. I wiped sweat from my forehead with the sleeve of my shirt and headed toward Preston.

"What's up, man? You ready?" I asked.

"How're you, Mr. Bishop?" The man in the navy blazer held his hand out. "I'm Winn Davis from Georgetown University."

I shook his hand. "How you doing?" I asked.

"I've been watching you play since you were in middle school—eighth grade, to be exact." He giggled. "You're an exceptional player."

"Thanks."

"Have you decided where you're going to college?"

"Not exactly." I hadn't really given college much thought. I thought that I'd take my time and figure things out. I wasn't sure if I'd pursue a career in sports or one in acting. I had options, and I still had time.

"When you get a chance, why don't you schedule a tour of our campus?" He pulled a business card out of his inside jacket pocket. "We'd love to fly you out to D.C. and show you around our campus. Maybe you can even check out a game while you're there."

I took the card. "Thanks. I'll give it some thought."

"Great meeting you, Drew." He smiled and then took a look around at all of my friends who had gathered. "You all have a nice evening."

As Winn Davis walked to his car, I pulled my hoodie over my head; grabbed my basketball from Malik.

"Drew, that was a scout!" Malik exclaimed. "You going to Georgetown?"

"I don't know, man," I said. "I might go to Julliard or somewhere that I can cultivate my acting skills."

"Acting skills?" asked Andre. "Man, you still on that acting trip? How you gon' go to the NBA if you running around trying to be Shakespeare?"

"I don't know, man. But I love the stage," I said and started walking toward Preston's car; motioned for him to come along.

"You coming back to play tomorrow, Big D?" asked Malik, calling me by my father's nickname.

"I might," I told him.

"Can I be on your team again?"

"If I come back tomorrow, yeah, you can be on my team," I told him.

The gleam in his eye was priceless. Malik Tucker had looked up to me since he first saw me play three years ago. He was ten at the time. And now, at age thirteen, he thought I was his idol. It felt good having a kid look up to me like that; gave me confidence. The scout who I'd just met also gave me confidence. It was good to know that I still had what it took to catch the eye of one of the best colleges in the nation.

Suddenly, I was a little unsure of myself. As I sank into the passenger's seat in Preston's car, I wondered if I'd made the right decision—transferring to Premiere.

twenty-one

Marisol

The room was decorated in silver and red balloons and streamers. So many trays filled with hot wings and pans of pizza were situated around the room. Huge television screens were mounted all over the walls. The music was blaring. Selena Gomez's voice filled the room and hundreds of kids danced to the music. I could've sworn I was dreaming, so I asked Luz to pinch me, just to make sure. She did.

"Ouch! Not that hard," I told her.

"Mari, this is beyond imagination," she said as she grabbed my wrist and pulled me through the crowd. "I could never have dreamed this in a million years."

A dark-haired Hispanic boy approached us. "You want to dance?"

I thought he was talking to Luz until I looked up and his dark eyes were staring straight into mine.

"Me?" I asked.

"Unless you don't like that song," he said.

The truth was, I loved Selena Gomez and I was really feeling the song. I bounced out onto the dance floor. My dark-haired partner kept up with my moves and we danced in the center of the crowded dance floor. He was very handsome in his blue jeans and white T-shirt with a vest. He wore a tan fedora on his head, and I instantly thought of Drew when I saw it.

Drew—my good friend back home in New York. The one who made me laugh when I didn't even feel like smiling. The boy who made me nervous when I shouldn't be. The one who I could have a conversation with for hours without end—about everything. The one who I'd forgotten all about until that moment. I'd forgotten to call or text when I'd made it to Los Angeles. There had been too much excitement for one day, but I knew he would understand. Besides, who had time to focus on New York, when Los Angeles was the place to be?

After a late night of dancing, Luz and I retired to our room. We'd grabbed snacks from the hotel's gift shop— Cool Ranch Doritos, Snickers bars, boxes of Red Hots, Lemonheads and Skittles—and dumped them all on the coffee table in the living room. We removed the cushions from the sofa sleeper and the sheets and blankets from all the beds; created a makeshift bed right there in the middle of the living room floor. Dressed in Victoria's Secret pajamas, we sat in the center of the floor and reminisced about our fairy-tale night until our eyelids were too heavy to keep opened.

The next morning, the telephone rang at seven o'clock and shook me out of my sleep. I stumbled over to the desk and fumbled around until I found the phone; picked up the receiver. The voice on the other end of the phone was that of a recording; a woman's voice stated that she was giving us a courtesy wake-up call. I carefully placed the receiver back into its cradle and stood there for a moment; gathered myself. It was so early, and we'd stayed up so late talking and laughing about everything.

"Luz," I whispered.

She didn't budge; just mumbled something in her sleep.

"Luz." I said it louder this time.

She barely opened her eyes—tried to focus on me. "Is it time to get up already?" she asked.

"It's time," I said and then headed for the bathroom; started the shower.

Today was going to be a good day.

A tour was the first order of business at Universal Studios. We toured the set of Steven Spielberg's movie *War of the Worlds* and took photos in front of the Bates Motel from the classic movie *Psycho*. After the tour, we made our way to the production studio where our movie's dance auditions were being held. The five of us were nervous, because we knew that only one of us would wind up dancing on the big screen. Four of us would be heading home on Sunday morning and back to a normal way of living. The dreams of four of us would come to a screeching halt very soon, and we all knew it.

I stood onstage in front of the producers of the film. The

music began to resonate through my body and I started moving to it; gave it my best shot. I danced better than I'd ever danced before. With a smile on my face, I took a bow as the music ended.

"Next!" yelled one of the producers.

That was my cue to exit the stage. I stepped down from the platform and took a seat next to Luz. The last contestant, Todd, took his place on the stage. The same song that I'd danced to began to play and Todd's body began to move to the beat. His routine was different from mine and the other three girls'. It was unique and could be described as almost perfect.

"Cut the music," one of the male producers yelled. "This is the guy…this is the one."

What was he saying? That Todd had made the cut?

"You're in, kid. You're the one," the female producer said. "Why don't you head on over to makeup. Let's get him in costume," she yelled to someone who whisked Todd away.

The rest of us sat there speechlessly. There was no time to stew over it. It was just cut and dry—almost heartless. The powers that be had spoken. They had decided our fate in a matter of minutes. I felt sick in the pit of my stomach—as though someone had punched me in it. As if my world had come to a crashing end. I wanted to cry, but the tears wouldn't come. They were on the brink of falling, but wouldn't. Instead, my heart pounded uncontrollably, and I wished I could rewind the past five minutes of my life. Wished I could have another shot to prove that I was worthy of that role in the film. That Todd probably had a better night's sleep, considering he hadn't attended the party. I wished I could tell them that they'd made a dreadful mistake. It was me who should've been heading over to *makeup* and getting into *costume*. It wasn't supposed to end this way.

The ride back to the hotel was quiet. No one said anything except for Gloria, who asked if we were hungry. No one was hungry. We were all sad and hurt—four emotional wrecks.

"You should all be proud of yourselves for making it this far," Gloria said as we pulled into the circular drive of the hotel. "I know you're disappointed, but this isn't the end. You've all proven that you have what it takes to be stars. Someone once told me this...reach for the moon, and even if you miss, you'll still be amongst the stars. Each of you is still amongst the stars. You're all fantastic dancers."

We listened, but no one responded. Her intentions were good, but nothing she could say would make us feel any better. We all stepped out of the car and headed inside the hotel lobby.

"This is your last night in L.A. Let's make it one that you'll remember for the rest of your lives. Meet me in the lobby at five o'clock. I'm going to show you around the city."

Although we weren't in the mood for another tour, we all agreed to meet Gloria at the designated time. But for now, I just wanted to get to my room as quickly as possible; bury my head beneath the pillow and sleep the day away. When my phone buzzed once—a text message—the last thing I wanted to do was read it. And I didn't. I ignored it.

Luz and I stepped into our room. I grabbed a soda from the fridge and headed for one of the bedrooms. Luz headed for the opposite bedroom, and we each closed our doors. I drew the blinds and then fell into bed. I turned on the clock radio on my bedside table and found a local hip-hop radio station. DJ Khaled's voice filled the room with the words to the song "All I Do Is Win, Win, Win." How ironic. The words couldn't be any more wrong, and I quickly changed the station. Covering my head with the pillow, I prayed for sleep. I didn't have to pray long. Between jet lag and the three-hour time difference between New York and L.A., sleep managed to find me right away. I didn't even realize that I had missed Gloria's fantastic tour.

As the morning sunshine peeked inside my window and crept across my face, I struggled to open my eyes. I'd slept all afternoon and through the night without interruption. It was rest that I clearly needed. I picked up the remote control and flipped on the television. Searched for MTV and tried to catch an episode of *Jersey Shore* before packing my things. After glancing at the digital clock on the nightstand, I knew that our flight was scheduled to leave within a few hours, and we were homeward-bound. I was ready to go home. There was nothing left for me in Hollywood except for heartache.

twenty-two

Drew

BEING inside a Broadway theater was nothing new for me. I'd been to plenty of shows and seen my share of off-Broadway and off-off-Broadway stage plays with my dad. It was those times with him that ignited the small fire beneath me; made me want to be on that stage instead of in the audience—an observer. Never had I been a member of the cast; backstage waiting for the curtains to go up.

The first scene—it's a Friday morning on the South Side of Chicago, sometime after World War II. The Youngers' living area is small. As a family, they live in the ghetto and they're poor. In fact, they share one bathroom with other tenants in an apartment house, and my son Travis sleeps on the sofa. The entire play is about the disappointment, false hope and despair of an African-American family in Chicago. The ending is almost depressing, and I felt sorry for the family we were portraying.

As I glanced out into the audience, I spotted Gram in the front row just as she'd promised. She was all smiles as she watched me work my magic. I could tell that she was proud. Preston sat next to her on the left—his eyes glued to the stage; probably thinking about how cute Asha was. The seat to Gram's right belonged to my father. It was empty, but I didn't sweat it. I finished my lines for the first scene and took a bow with the rest of my classmates as the curtains were drawn.

We all rushed backstage and quickly changed clothes in preparation for the next scene. I thought about my father; wondered why he hadn't shown up. Before he'd left for work, I told him that there would be a ticket at the box office for him. He said he'd do all he could to make it. I was hopeful at first, but was discouraged when I didn't see him sitting next to Gram in the audience. I wanted my dad to respect my love for the stage, and how could he do that if he never saw me act?

As I prepared myself to go back out there, I resigned myself to the fact that he probably wouldn't show up. In order to get through the scenes, I had to block it from my mind. It was okay. Even though the visit from the basketball scout had me off course for a moment, I knew that acting was my true love. And with that, I knew I had to pursue it, whether my dad supported it or not. I had to do what was best for me—what made me happy.

Dressed in a white dress shirt, a black tie and black slacks, I went back onstage. I was confident about my lines and gave them everything I had. I was in the zone before long. We all bounced our lines off one another until the end of the scene. We'd nailed it, and I was proud to be a part of the cast. As we took a bow, the audience stood and clapped. It was then that I noticed Dad in the front row—right next to Gram, smiling and clapping as if he'd lost his mind. It was a happy moment.

twenty-three

Marisol

Our entire neighborhood stood in the middle of the street as our town car pulled up in front of Luz's house. We smiled at each other, thinking that all of our friends and neighbors had gathered to welcome us home. They were proud of us, we thought, even though we wouldn't be appearing in any films anytime soon. However, as it turned out, they weren't gathered for us at all. As we stepped out of the car, it appeared that something serious was going on.

Stacking our luggage at the curb, our driver bid us farewell and took off in the opposite direction of the crowd. Luz and I approached the group, and I spotted Grace in the middle of it.

"Oh, my God. Mari! Luz!" Grace exclaimed and rushed our way. She gave us both a big hug.

A few people followed Grace, and with everyone trying to explain what was going on, I wasn't able to understand anyone clearly.

"I can't hear everyone at once," I said.

Kristina emerged from the crowd. "Mari, it's Nico. He has a gun!"

I wasn't surprised about the gun; I'd seen Nico's gun before I left for Los Angeles. I rushed toward the center of the crowd; found Nico standing there—pointing the gun at Diego.

"I'm tired of watching my back!" said Nico as his hand shook. "I don't want to be a part of your gang, or any other gang!"

Diego stood there, staring at Nico; unmoved. He didn't seem to be afraid of the gun that was pointed his way. Instead, he slapped Nico's shaky hand, and the gun hit the pavement with a loud thud. The two of them raced for the gun, and before I knew it, they were rolling around on the ground. A shot rang out, and I was paralyzed. I couldn't move. One of them had been shot—Nico or Diego—I wasn't sure which one. I stood there with both hands covering my mouth.

What a way to be welcomed home.

In the back of the ambulance, Mami held on to Nico's left hand. With an IV in his right hand, he was scared. I could tell. It was like the time when we thought the bogeyman was hiding in our closet, and we sat there with our backs against the wall waiting for him to show his ugly face. With fear in our eyes, we waited, but he never showed up. It was the same fear that I saw in Nico's eyes now. Tears crept down the side of his face. My vision was blurred with tears of my own as Poppy squeezed my hand.

I wasn't sure which part of Nico's body the bullet had struck, but I knew that he was losing blood. Quickly. I thought of Diego. There had been fear in his eyes, too. The gun had fired accidentally as the two of them had struggled with it. He stood there afterward, not knowing if he should run for his life or make sure that his old friend was alive. He had been torn.

"I wasn't trying to shoot him," he said and looked straight into my eyes as I held him in my arms, his blood smeared all over my white shirt.

I truly believed that Diego hadn't meant for the gun to go off. But it had, and my brother was shot. And there was nothing that Diego or anyone else could do about it. As sirens rang out from a nearby neighborhood, he'd finally made the ultimate decision to take off running. He was gone before the paramedics and the police arrived. I could hear our friends and neighbors explaining the incident to the police and saw them pointing the officers in the direction that Diego had run.

Once at Lutheran Medical Center, my parents and I found ourselves pacing the floor of the intensive care unit's waiting room. As my father sipped on coffee from a foam cup, my mother held on to her rosary beads and closed her eyes. I imagined that she was praying, which I thought was a pretty good idea. I'd prayed in the ambulance on the way over, but mine hadn't lasted quite that long. I slouched in my seat and checked my text messages that I hadn't gotten around to looking at since Saturday. I'd been too busy wallowing in my own depression over the competition. But now as I sat there worrying about my brother, my troubles didn't seem so bad.

Hey M…how did it go? Jasmine's text read.

I didn't make it. Todd did.

Did you have fun?

Lots.

That's all that matters.

Jasmine was right. All that mattered was that I had a great time. I got to spend the weekend in L.A. I went to a great Hollywood party—teen party, that is. I toured Universal Studios and got to dance in front of a real live film producer. After looking at it that way, I knew that I hadn't handled it right. Here Jasmine was on the other end of my phone, and she'd missed out on all of that and still had a great attitude.

How's UR dad?

Recovering.

Good news!!

I quit smoking!

Seriously?

Yes!

That was great news. Since the day I met Jasmine, I'd hoped that she would quit that terrible habit.

Why did u quit?

My dad almost died. No mas. Didn't kno that smoking could cause heart disease.

Proud of U.

Where R U?

Lutheran. My brother was shot.

??

Crazy day.

I'm coming over there!

I knew that Jasmine was serious when she showed up at the hospital, her little brother Xavier in tow. She gave both my parents a hug and then hugged me. The two of us sat there and got caught up on everything. Just talking to her helped me to take my mind off Nico, if only for a moment. That is, until the gray-haired doctor in a white coat stepped through the automatic doors and approached my parents. He had news about Nico.

"Mr. and Mrs. Garcia?

"Yes," Poppy stood. Gave the doctor a firm handshake.

"Your son is going to be okay."

Those words did my heart good; calmed my fears.

"The bullet missed his lung and we think that we'll be able to get to it with ease. But we need to act quickly. I'd like to send him into emergency surgery right away…"

I exhaled. My brother was going to be fine. I guessed God had heard Mami's and my prayers, and I was grateful.

THE FALL SOCIAL

twenty-four

Marisol

LUZ put the last little curl in my hair while Kristina applied my makeup. I felt like a princess as I sat there in my no-nonsense little black dress with the halter-style neck. Jesse and I had decided on red and black as our colors. After much begging and agreeing to bring my American history grade back up, I was allowed to attend the fall social. My parents actually agreed that Jesse could pick me up at our house.

After Nico's brush with death, my parents were feeling a lot more merciful. My mother had finally loosened her grip a little, and I was glad. I hated that it had taken my brother's injury to make her more easygoing. I also hated that he'd had to endure the pain of a gunshot wound, simply because he didn't want to join a gang. How many ways did he have to say it before it registered with Diego and his posse? They'd forced his hand and caused him to think that his only means for survival was to carry a gun. A gun that almost took his life. I believed that because he hadn't backed down to Diego that he'd earned the respect that he deserved. So, it seemed that the gun had also saved his life.

His body was healing fine after the surgery. But that was more than I could say for his mouth.

"I don't care how much makeup you put on her, she's still going to look like the Wicked Witch of the West," he said, sticking his head into my bedroom.

"Shut up, Nico!" said Grace.

"He knows that you look good, Chica," Luz said. "That's why he's got his nose all up in your bedroom."

"Why is he even in here?" asked Grace.

"Isn't there something you should be doing?" asked Kristina.

"Um…in case you haven't noticed, I can barely walk," Nico said. "Otherwise, I'd be outside whipping your brother in a game of hoops."

"Can you tell Mami to come here, Nico?" I asked.

"Mami!" he yelled. "Mari wants you!"

"I could've done that," I told him.

"I hope you didn't expect me to hobble down that flight of stairs and bring her up here," he said.

"No. Of course not." I gave him a fake grin.

I heard Mami's footsteps in the stairwell, and soon she appeared in the doorway. "Look at you, *mi hija!* You look beautiful."

"You think so?" I asked her.

"I know so," she said. "Now you should get a move on. Your date's here."

Grace, Kristina, Luz and I all rushed over to my bedroom window and looked outside. Everyone wanted to catch of glimpse of Jesse Lucas in his tuxedo, or at least a glimpse of his car. A beautiful, silver Mercedes was parked in front of my house, while its handsome driver was downstairs being interrogated by my father. I needed to go rescue him.

"What's he wearing?" I asked Mami.

"A very nice black tuxedo, but…" She hesitated.

"But what?"

"He's wearing sneakers…with a tux," she said and frowned. "And he's wearing a silly black hat on his head."

"He's wearing a hat?"

"What kind of hat?" Grace asked with a frown.

"What's that silly hat called?" She thought for a moment. "A fedora."

"He's wearing a fedora?" I asked.

I had to see this. I took one last glance at myself in the mirror and then straightened my dress. Headed for the stairs; took them slowly down—careful not to trip over my feet. At the bottom of the stairs, my date stood there with a wide grin on his face. Instead of a carnation, he held a single, long-stemmed rose in his hand.

"Wow," he said when he saw me.

"What did you do with my date?" I asked Drew.

I couldn't help but smile; I was so glad to see him. With the competition and all the drama that had gone on with Nico, I hadn't seen Drew much. And I missed him. He looked handsome in his black tuxedo, black high-top

Converses and black fedora. I couldn't help but stare. It had been a great compliment—being asked to the dance by the most gorgeous guy in school, Jesse Lucas. But all I really wanted in the first place was for Drew Bishop to ask me.

"I *am* your date." He smiled.

"Where's Jesse? Did you stuff him in the trunk of your car or something?" I had to ask.

"I told him that the dance had been postponed until next week," Drew said and laughed. "I'm kidding. I was a gentleman and asked if he minded if I took you to the dance."

"You did?"

"No, but who cares about all that? You're stuck with me, kid." He handed me the rose and held his arm out for me to take hold of it. "You ready or what?"

I feared that I would never find out the truth about my original date.

"Yes, I'm ready," I said.

I gave Mami a kiss on the cheek; then Poppy. "I love you both."

"Drew and I have already discussed your curfew," Poppy stated as he gave Drew a stare. "You remember, right, Drew?"

"Yes, sir. I do."

"So this is the infamous Drew." Luz pushed her way past Kristina and Grace. She held her hand out to him. "I'm Luz, Mari's best friend."

Drew took her hand in his. "Good to meet you."

"He's a cutie," said Grace.

"Does he have any brothers?" Kristina asked.

"Let me get a picture." Mami grabbed her disposable camera and started snapping shots of us.

"It's time to go," I said to Drew and then grabbed his arm and ushered him out the door.

I couldn't wait to get inside the beautiful silver car. I pretended that it was my chariot and I was Cinderella. Drew held the door of the Mercedes open for me. I stepped inside and sunk into the leather seat. As soon as he started the engine, an old-school rap song by Doug E. Fresh filled the car. I listened to the words as Drew slowly pulled the car away from the curb.

"Is this your car?" I asked.

"Yes. I call her Delilah," he said.

"Delilah?" I asked. "You're so funny."

"I know."

He took his hat off, laid it on the backseat of the car. "Mind if I let the top down?"

"Now?" I asked. "It's cold outside!"

"It's fifty-two degrees."

Although fifty-two degrees was a lot warmer than most fall days in New York, it was still pretty chilly. But I didn't care. Being with Drew managed to warm my heart. The car's convertible top came down, and my hair began to blow in the wind.

"Luz is gonna kill me about my hair," I told him.

"She'll get over it."

Drew turned up the volume on the stereo. As some song called "La-Di-Da-Di" began to play, Drew bounced in his seat. As he merged the car onto the Brooklyn-Queens Expressway, I-278, I knew that tonight would not be like any other night in my life.

★ ★ ★ ★ ★

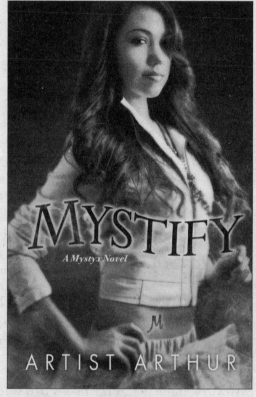

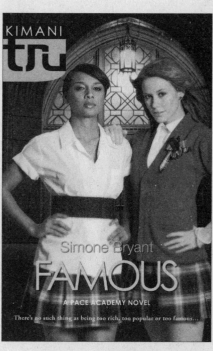